D0377555

MOVIEOLA!

Generously Donated By

Richard A. Freedman

Trust

Albuquerque / Bernalillo County Library

Also by John Domini

MOVIEOLA!

stories by

JOHN DOMINI

3907505177321

db
DZANC
BOOKS

DZANC
BOOKS

5220 Dexter Ann Arbor Rd.
Ann Arbor, MI 48103
www.dzancbooks.org

The characters and events in this book are fictitious. Any similarity to real persons, living or dead, is coincidental and not intended by the author.

MOVIEOLA!. Copyright © 2016, text by John Domini. All rights reserved, except for brief quotations in critical articles or reviews. No part of this book may be reproduced in any manner without prior written permission from the publisher: Dzanc Books, 5220 Dexter Ann Arbor Rd., Ann Arbor, MI 48103.

Cover image: "The Grand Sampler," by Frank Hansen (Moberg Gallery, Des Moines, IA). Photo by Camille Renee.

Designed by Steven Seighman

These stories, in somewhat different form, appeared previously in *Caketrain*, *The Collagist*, *Conjunctions, elimae, Gargoyle, Keyhole, The Literary Review, Puerto del Sol*, and elsewhere. I'm grateful to the editors, and to everyone else who helped, in particular Lettie Prell.

Library of Congress Cataloging-in-Publication Data

Names: Domini, John, 1951- author.Title: Movieola : short stories / by John Domini.Description: First edition. | Ann Arbor, MI : Dzanc Books, 2016.Identifiers: LCCN 2015033331 | ISBN 9781938103902 (paperback) Subjects: | BISAC: FICTION / Short Stories (single author). | FICTION / Literary. | FICTION / Humorous. | FICTION / Satire.Classification: LCC PS3554.O462 A6 2016 | DDC 813/.54--dc23LC record available at http://lccn.loc.gov/2015033331

First U.S. Edition: June 2016

Printed in the United States of America

10 9 8 7 6 5 4 3 2 1

Early exemplars: Anne, George, Jack, Don, Stanley.

TABLE OF CONTENTS

MOVIEOLA!

Mothers of America
            let your kids go to the movies!
get them out of the house so they won't know what you're up to
it's true that fresh air is good for the body
                        but what about the soul
that grows in darkness, embossed by silvery images

— FRANK O'HARA

MAKING THE TRAILER

For the opening we go with The Arrival of the Hit Men. That's the way to make a trailer, a hundred seconds or so of grabber screentime: start with killers in an airport. No need to be crass about it. No need for any kind of race thing, religion thing, politics thing. Pure fear, that's what we want, the lowdown cello throb like someone's pulling a bow right across the spinal column. And what are you watching? A couple of adorable kids holding hands, waiting at the metal detector, and some clean-cut Homeland Security gunman giving them a worry-free smile (works best if the kids are white, the soldier black)...but meanwhile, behind them, in just-perceptible slo-mo, two guys whose getup screams *Made*. Made men and vain about it, in their long, pomade-heavy hair, their knee-length closet-creased black leather coats (belt, no zipper; no faggy excess). Of course they've got their sunglasses on too, even as they emerge from the ramp into JFK or O'Hare.

The arrival of the hit men, the first six seconds, seven seconds, and just like that, everyone in the theater's into some madness they can never make sense of. The story hook's sunk so deep even Ebert himself couldn't spit it out. One of the killers has acne scars, a pocked and webbed jawline to suggest his soul's compromises, and to give his victim a good scare to go on—the last face you'll see. Let's get their reflections too. Let's use that floor-to-ceiling security partition, a wan Plexiglas mirror that catches the darker glimmer of their twinned Ray-Bans. See them looming behind a couple scotch-for-lunch businessmen in sloppy lowhung slacks. A foxy young mom wouldn't hurt either, cooing over her baby while she's wearing nightclub lipstick. Yes, that's Hook Number One: a shadow of the shadow-bringers.

Number Two, we can't make this trailer without the Aging Rock Star Recording with a Gospel Choir. Nothing will do except a beer-faced forty- or fifty-something, his small pale hand disappearing inside the darker paws of the choir leader for Something-or-Other Baptist Church. Yes, what a grip on that choir leader! He's got both hands into his greeting, and his paired fists are as humped and black as a gun bulging under a leather jacket. We'll need maybe five seconds just for that handshake, that shared smile; let the cameras wheel around both men. The rocker's smile isn't quite there yet, a grimace as shapeless as windblown cocaine, no way to connect the dots. But not many people can claim teeth and cheekbones like his new fig-brown friend, the kind of smile that made him a natural to play "Choir Leader." A Satchmo smile, box-framed by a strong Ashanti face. It fills the screen while the actual leader hides behind the organ in her bifocals and dentures, her early-Aretha process.

Hey, we know what a choir leader's supposed to look like. The man we picked, what's so great about his high-intensity beaming is the way it's set off by all that's out of focus behind him, the actual leader plus the rest of the singers. Their faces lurk like brown outgrowths (though don't forget the lipstick) atop their purple robes. Everyone glitters obscurely under the halogen lamps. More shadow, see? In the airport or behind the smile, we always give our audience that smear of the dark.

Hold the handshake till whitey's own grinning improves. Because it does improve; he's thinking of a comeback. In fact the star's earlier Top Forty number might work for us, a few bars anyway, a few low strokes of the cello sketching out an old prom ballad. We'll get the guys in Music on it, some weeper as sloppy as the adult-fit slacks the rock star has to wear these days. So then as the shot culminates with the so-called choir leader, the so-called star will go all twinkle, twinkle again, thinking what kind of advance the company might be good for. He needs a good-sized chunk of change to pay off Rat the Scumbag. And he's heard that Rat the Scumbag has run out of patience and called in a couple of bad guys.

From there it's straight to the chorus of the new number, the so-called singer-songwriter out front with his guitar (a big full-bodied thing to hide his gut), while behind him we keep that hint of blur working, the choir out of focus. Everyone's into the tune of course, swaying and clapping. We can't go so soft-focus that we don't see the leader and his Satchmo smile again as some key phrase rises, a couple of words like "I know," or rather *ahuhyiii-yiiii nyuh-nyuh-ohhh*. Then we catch the star really smiling. Really, he's smiling, and not just because he's thinking of something new for the Top Forty, something "with a bullet." It's like a fresh *a-yi-yi* out of the warrior brave you thought was killed during some previous fight choreography; it's a moment when the guy's heart, more than half-pickled and way over-pampered, has been restored to its proper exercise and joy. There's a better climax coming after all. Anything's possible.

Though the singer out front never casts a glance behind him. No. That's not possible. Nobody cares about the choir and their undulations. We'll leave that ripple and eddy soft-focus: the shipwreck behind us.

Plus, what kind of a flick would this be without the Happy Lesbian Couple at Home? Got to get that in here, a pair of slender late risers around the kitchen counter, bantering and kissyface, in great lipstick. Two blondes work best, two shades of blonde, one the dark of a tinted window, the other glimmering like silk under a lamp. That second girl, Glimmer-Hair, styles hers hetero, a housewife cut, but she's also got one of those macho scoop-&-strap undershirts. The sort of undershirt a hit man would wear. Our movie's not too PG to prevent the girlfriend, Tint-Hair, from taking advantage of that undershirt a little, yanking on the scoop to reveal, over the heart, the blossom of some long-stemmed tattoo. Now if the blossom's over the heart, then the root must be.... But there's no need to be crass about it. Just the opposite; this is the sympathy moment. We've got to catch just the right beat of the dialogue too. Got to make sure that everybody out there watching knows that everybody who made this movie knows that, whenever these two take a break from sucking on each other's cunts, they're just the same as the rest of us.

So the bright Formica, the glitter of banter, the hefty Starbucksware. When the darker blonde starts stretching for her run, her slit shorts are as pretty as the eggs and fruit. Out in the seats everyone gets a tick or two of comfort, in the sunshine that glides over the flimsy fabric that glides over those taut…those pert…. Everyone gets a moment for this slick-&-happy, and they can take it as far as they'd like, maybe even beyond the sex. Anything's possible. Somebody might even go beyond these bodies in their packaging and get to a hint of happiness itself. Happiness, that undetectable fetus which kicks and stretches inside the sex.

Whatever. It's only a beat, and then we spring the next stinger: these girls are taking revenge on their ex-boyfriend. Their ex the aging rock star, the man who first got this twosome together for a threesome.

Takes no more than a mention of the threebie, the least snip of a word and a glance. With that we go right for the craw: these girls are getting their former third party back but good. They've got him in the hole to Rat the Scumbag. We don't need details, connect the dots. All we need, for the folks out in the seats, we gave them already. We gave them that first glimpse of the rock star's face. That powder-strewn vacancy, *I like to watch.*

Spring the news and cut, bang, to the Artist Going to Hell with an Inappropriate Girlfriend. And the first we screen these two, everyone out in the seats has to be kept guessing; our audience slams from sunshine to *noir*, from a couple they've come to know to another they can only wonder about. We have all this ready-made packaging, now terror now tits, we should use it. Shuffle and deal again, and let's keep a clock in the frame too, one of those neon bar clocks on which all you can see are hands and shadow. Likewise our "artist," our "girlfriend"—over the next few seconds they're familiar only in the sense of a re-iterated gesture, a hand in the shadow. A man of promise is getting led astray by some sex-o-lette. Her outfit shows plenty of skin, her lipstick's good and bright but smeared a bit, and our virtuoso-in-collapse slouches on his stool, in a heap of black leather, a long black leather jacket mostly undone, with a belt, no zipper...

Now the audience catches on, even as the camera keeps the twosome off-center, the shot focused on the bar's booze puddles and cellophane crumples, the glimmer of reflected neon. It's a shipwreck. When the grr, grr, grrrl licks our hit man's face, it's like an oil fire on the roiled ocean surface. Yes, and now the closeup on the scars along the man's jawline, the pocked and webbed leftovers of his compromises. Yes, and now too no one can fail to real-ize that they've seen the girl before. They recognize the décolletage, very scoop-&-strap; they see the tattoo rose between her boobs. If the blossom's up there, then what kind of thorns are down below? Oh yeah, that'll snag every eyeball out there. They love it when the madness returns, the triple-cross heebie-jeebies, the hook twisting to grab yet another long-familiar mindset. And our hit man had so much potential! He was no mere rock star, but a true artist, a shooter of unparalleled gifts. But now look at him. She's got him talking too much.

Look, he says, *the way it's supposed to work...*

That's good, thataway—but look, what are we doing making trailers in the first place? What, if not to really drive them out of their minds in the last ten seconds? So we zap them with a departure from form. An experiment. The critics go crazy for that kind of thing, when the buzz starts among the tech people, and what we do is, we go to a kind of kiss. A larger-than-life kiss, extreme closeup: *we put just the guy's mouth up there.* The way a mouth looks, up there surrounded by the dark, it's very weird, it's a great gimmick. Something fetal in its folds and balances. Then the man, his mouth, starts listing the ways his artistry is supposed to work. He mentions: By the Roadside in Long Island, with the Statue of Liberty in the distance and some Italian pastry on the seat. Afterwards you leave the murder weapon, but take the pastry. *Take the cannoli,* he says; that's how the job's supposed to be done. You begin with the most weary, stale, flat sort of cliché, the shadow of death, and then with the right kind of work in the kitchen you make it otherwise.

And those Lips Above, a prodigy you would never think could be contained in so flat a surface, bring up another one: Gunning Down the Rich and Amoral Sham who Stole Your Child Lover. For that you first make your victim read aloud a kind of love song, a poem you've composed about the difference between your own pedophilia and his. You need to get drunk, too, and not just on liquor, but on all the impossible promise in American hugs and kisses, highways and movies. That's a lo-lo-lovely one. But there are lots of others, and this man knows them all.

It's such a great gimmick, those lips, this list. It's going to set off a wild buzz, maybe even give rise to a whole new generation of coming attractions—especially since every-body watching won't have any idea what happens next. Does the hit go to hell? Does the other lovergirl appreciate the old switcheroo? There's no way of knowing, and you can't take your eyes from those vast human folds just up ahead, as they squeeze out yet another possibility (still per-fectly audible, though a gospel choir has started to rise be-hind the dialogue): the one where You Pour Poison in the Ear of the Sleeping King. You have to choose a moment when the queen seems ripe for a fresh bedmate and the prince, always trouble, is away at school. God, the surprises in a great trailer! The twists and turns! We've nailed it now, we've changed the connections inside every cerebral cortex out there, and the choir hammers its rhythms home with ever more power, and there's no longer any telling how the kill might go, in all its fertility…. Then the name.

ASSASSINS, STORYBOARDS TO DATE

What we have so far is, we begin with the down-to-earth, the romance angle, a girl who's about to give up on finding a decent guy, she figures it'll never get anywhere, the games never end. Begin where anyone can make the connection, that's the whole first board, just another girl sick of the same-old, all the more of a drag because she knows what she's got to offer, she's old enough to know but she's still good-looking, sure, hot when she wants to be, and she's had a life, boyfriends, maybe girl-friends, maybe put a little edge on her, plus she's got degrees on the wall and they say she's some kind of doer of science, and she's got a lab, that's important. We could go as old as thirty-five. The point is, when she gets it going with this guy, our guy, that's got to line up nice and natural with the romance, it's got to feel like this is it, the boyfriend she's been waiting for, and all we need to suggest the trouble, I mean our principal twist, the fact that he's a highly trained secret government assassin—the only hint we need for that here at the start is the right shadows during the meet.

We're thinking a bookstore meet, a place like that we kill two birds with one stone, we establish brains and a basis, I mean the basis between our guys, we were thinking maybe poetry, the stiff that dreams are made on. Oh, it's *stuff*? The stuff that dreams are made in, whatever, Google, the point is that's what drives the meet, and our girl's so taken by this sweet guy, he's got the poetry and he's got the abs, we'll put him in a snug white T, and she's so bowled over she doesn't notice the shadows. For this we see some way-high old-time bookstore shelves so his face is all in shadow, our girl never sees him clearly, she never has a clue about how this great new guy spent a couple of years up at the Compound, Fatal Blows 101 through the Seminar in Body Disposal, and after that he did at least a couple more rotations out in the alleyway, the parking garage, the uppermost window of a little-used warehouse. Carrying a high-powered rifle with a laser scope. Carrying a short black Beretta with a long silver silencer, whatever, flashbacks, carrying a page of boxscores on which the ink conducts an electric charge that induces heart seizure. Carrying a condom lubricated with a penetrating toxic gel—but not for our girl, no, she's not a target, it's the real deal between these two and we can never lose sight of that, it's our bottom-line arc. For the two of them every orgasm's as distinct and gorgeous as a snowflake.

That's why we can't have her see him kill somebody, either, or not first thing, not for her first irrefutable clue of what her new perfect sweetie does for a living. First would be something like this next board here, she discovers this strange condom and she goes all horrified thinking maybe he's cheating, but then she's not the usual helpless woman wronged, I mean who *might* be wronged, remember the degrees, remember the lab, a roomful of white oblong apparatus each with its own blinking red light, and so she can stay late one night and establish scientifically whether this man who she believed was a true and immutable boyfriend was instead just more of the same-old. She's got latex gloves and the latest technology in chemical analysis, plus the kind of heart you need to ride herd on all those knobs and buttons, but next thing you know it turns out this girl's going to need the heart of a saber-toothed tiger, a mama saber-toothed tiger, because she's sitting over a lethal condom, right there between the clips of her trace analyzer, and she's learned the truth, science doesn't lie, her guy might be highly trained but he's no longer so secret. And with that she signals some kind of take-charge, snapping off the gloves or whipping out the ponytail, thirty-fucking-five and she's ready to start all over. We can use the light here again, we see the lab with an entire wall of windows, sweatshop style with the iron frames, and at this moment practically white with sun in this glowing visual metaphor as what she must do burns through the boxes of her life to date and turns her into a total babe for a moment, showing cleavage under the smock while her eyelids flutter and lips go ajar, a woman in the middle of another snowflake, while she realizes this is the one and only real deal in her life and there's just one way to keep it, and that's to stand by her man, shoulder to shoulder, assassins together.

So then we're into the Compound, you see she's traded one smock for another, the karate uniforms the recruits

wear, and she's good in this outfit too, easy on the eyes and
nasty on her feet. Her trainers have reached the point of
pulling the criminally insane in off the streets for her, and
our girl handles every one of them, she faces off with some
Aryan Brotherhood musclehead and she flips him over one
shoulder and then freezes him with a slippered foot on his
tattooed throat, and then, whatever, split-screen, she kicks
the legs out from under some Shaq-sized OG and does
a knee drop into his groin, he's a jelly donut after that.
Finally some dry ice in a suit and tie eases into the room,
some alpha exec who watches our girl from between the
soundproofing baffles, and meanwhile she goes straight at
some Hell's Angels psycho with one of those stares like he
was born without eyelids, like he's four parts reptile, and
before we realize what's happened she blinds him with a
flick of her between-bouts talcum powder and then spins
him and, hunkering up against his back, isolates one of his
kidneys with razor-sharp steel-tipped nails. When the suit
steps out from behind the baffles he might allow himself
a bit of slow applause, that's the actor's prerogative, but in
the face this CO or whoever has got to remain the Ice-
Man, the Dry-Ice Man, and when he declares our girl is
field-ready it's got to come across without affect, a fore-
gone conclusion, karate doesn't lie, and what have we just
been watching if not one *highly* trained secret government
motherfucker?

Though after that the bossman takes a moment to show
off his own chops, finishing the girl's latest victim when
the biker with the lizard lids (and a brain to match) comes
out of his paralysis with a roar—no problem, or not for the
man with the corner office, not in this firm, and you can

barely follow as he whips off his striped tie and uses it a garrote. Don't mess with Wall Street! Then a moment later this old hand is thoroughly executive again, the Vice President in Charge of Asperse, and the light goes flat while he finds a mirror (maybe a pair of mirrored sunglasses off the big OG) to check the fresh knot in his tie, and with his back to our girl the CO gives her her first assignment. The kind of light we need here, it's so flat it turns the colors trashy, it's like for a training film, because for our girl it's all about going to school, suddenly, it's learning the hard way, as she hears about an agent breaking bad out there, a troubling case, a former top man who may even have gone rogue...

I mean, up at the Compound, a recruit can't have a boyfriend, can she? And see why we keep that information under wraps? If we'd sent our girl's new man back to school with her, then what would be left for the boards? We'd have two moves left, and after that all we could do is make sure we got the gaffer's name right in the credits, the first move would be "Pomp and Circumstance" and the second "Here Comes the Bride."

We can't leave our bottom line lying there, just lying there, not after we've gotten this far, and once our girl goes into training, think about it, she's got to keep her mind on higher things, in fact that's where the honchos in their suits and ties want her to keep her mind, her and all the other apprentice hitpersons, they want them all the time on task, and then on top of *that* there's how our former Miss Lonesome Tonight feels about the honey that got her here in the first place. A great boyfriend requires great sacrifice, a true girlfriend has to be born again, hardening the mind and humiliating the flesh, plus the flesh of a dozen or so bad guys in from the street. It's all there in the start, the romance, and once that's in place and the lighting's working, then anyone watching can make the connection, the things we'll do just to keep the orgasms up in the stratosphere, up where the water turns to crystal, and anyone can feel what the girl feels when the first man she's ordered to kill is her man, the bod from the bookstore, the stuff that made guys dream on.

You see how we need the surprise, through this part? We need a twist or two under wraps, unless we're going to return to Square One, and it's beautiful the way it works through this part, because what did he know, the boyfriend, the first killer onscreen, what did *he* know about his girl's sacrifice? All he has is her smock on the laboratory floor and some hard-to-figure traces in the apparatus, and now we see him shedding tears over those red lights, they go on blinking but it's just not the same, and he's even weeping over the keyboard as he uses her credit card to charge a few high-ticket items, identity theft usually flushes out the actual cardholder. But the only phone calls that come in are pitches for debt consolidation, the recorded voices always a few seconds out of, out of, out of sync, and soon enough our man's that way himself, off-kilter, because whatever his deal is, this part was real for him too, and when he's up in another warehouse window with the rifle in his hands suddenly he can't tell the infrared crosshairs from the nearest bar neon, *Ladies 2 for 1*, and he's started to grind fresh green bud into his poison-filtered cigarettes and then tear off the filters and smoke the things himself: a secretly trained high government assassin. The last time he used the condom he almost put it on inside out.

That was probably Management's mistake, that one, somebody higher up hadn't thought it through, asking the man to go fuck someone else, but now they're setting things straight, the Ice Brothers at the top, they're giving the assignment to their nastiest new graduate, terrific promise even if she is a little old. As for the lighting, at this point we want as much as we can get, too much technically speaking, we want it so you can't see our girl's face or the CO's except when first one and then the other steps, in profile, into the glare of the lamp, one of those blinding white halogens set above the barbed wire somewhere, we want that visual metaphor too, asking, are these faces alike or what?, who's the killer who's the lover?, and then right away, bang, while that quandary's still in your mind's eye we go straight to black on black, our girl in a commando ninja jumpsuit and ski cap skittering down the mountainside from the Compound's exit, itself camouflaged, everything on the screen as invisible as her thinking, which by now has hatched a plan to save her guy. She hasn't spent all this time up here in the Fortress of Kick Ass just to come back down to street level with a very different sort of heart, the heart of a Gila monster, and now she pauses in the dark to pull out some piece of ID, bright white, entirely official, maybe she can click a nail against its edge, and there's a photo on the card, a familiar face, the sweetheart below. That's all it takes to make the connection, to make sense of that time she spent chatting up the impressionable young clerk in the Records Office, learning his birthday and his favorite ballclub and his mother's maiden name, and then that time when the clerk let our girl "hang out" in the office while he ran an errand down to D Level and as soon as his back was turned she snapped on a pair of latex gloves.

We see it all now. Except unfortunately that includes the leathery and unsmiling CO, him too, he's traded in his suit and tie for the no-see-um PJs, and of course he's long suspected, our girl could never get black enough to hide from the bossman, so he's got to clamber down the mountain behind her, ready to undo everything he and his people have done for her, because it's not just about the girl, it's also about the target, the agent who's started to lose it, or to look like he's losing it. Because in fact the guy might've gone rogue. That's what her CO had been trying to tell this girl up in the Romper Room, it's the oldest twist in the business, don't talk to me about a real deal, it's one minute you look like a stone burnout and the next you're someone *else's* secret assassin, and still trained on this government's dollar. The very thought has the old-timer muttering to himself, if this bitch lives long enough to make exec she'll have seen it a thousand times, every day's the same when you spend them down in the pit, and here we'll use the moonlight, we'll catch just that oval around his eyes, the wrinkles avuncular, a frostlike radiation as he stares down the rocky outcroppings and the scree, muttering they all think they're bulletproof.

Which is about as far as we've got, except, no question, we're staying with our root arc, staying right where we started on the romance, though I guess we'll figure out what it comes down to in the end after the pre-screenings, I guess that's up to the usual strangers in the dark, good news bad news. Though we do have a panel here showing the girl has a plan to change his face, the boyfriend's, a plan to cut and paste, because for her it's not about anyone's face anymore, is it, not after all this time in the bowels of the mountain slashing through the scum of the earth—I ask you, what do lips and eyes and like that amount to, after you've been there and back, except some indistinct planes of light and shadow, a hand of Tarot that spells out a tale of love for a few staring moments and then gets swept off the table, destroyed, so that the cards can be reshuffled and then laid out again, in who knows what new confabulation? Everything's a secret and anything's possible. Plus finally we do have this one part here of in-the-meantime, this one bit of back in the world, with the guy, the boyfriend, the blade who could cut either way. We've got him doing what he can to fill the empty squares on the calendar, mixing up the Nestle's with rum, whatever, montage, laying out her camisole again and decorating it with the stray hairs he's found and kept safe, and studying his favorite Polaroid of her, that time he caught her just at climax, and standing before the mirror trying to mold his mouth to match her own ecstatic shape, somewhere between grin and yowl, trying to get it right by putting his fingers to the glass...

BOOKSTORES OF HOLLYWOOD

S he's heard all about it, visualization. Heard the talk and seen the email—if you want something to happen, you've first got to *visualize*—and yet she never expected anything like today. Never expected Industrial Light & Magic in a mall off one of the boulevards. Of course there are people in the industry who swear it's magic anyway, visualization; an image in the mind's eye, they'll tell you, is halfway to elephant dollars at the b.o. Even a picture of a picture can make all the difference, you frame your pitch with the right shot and you walk out of there with a quarter million in startup. And she's experimented, sure. At Starbucks for instance, during that comforting moment when your Venti's on the way, she's given the technique a whirl, she's kited off into a sky full of money shots. But never anything like today.

Not that she hasn't set herself apart already. She's hardly been in town a year, Nola, but she's worked out her niche:

the girl who talks the high end. Let the others talk demographics, the 18 to 25, let them talk distribution groupings and ROI. Nola would talk narrative, not story but *narrative*. Never mere closeups, but moments of recognition. A niche that fit, the art end, and she had the look for it, less LA pastel and more NYC black. Her hair boldface parentheses around angular hard-plastic glasses. A look like she's working toward a doctorate at the Sorbonne.

Her boyfriend loved it. The strategy, that is, that's what he loved, all that politicking stuff. He'd rather talk about the most powerful table position at a dinner party than the kind of "positions" most boyfriends liked to talk about—because what he really preferred, Nola was starting to think (talk about a picture within a picture), was boys. She wasn't sure. She wasn't going to snicker at his name, Gaylord. She had to admit he made a lip-smacking presentation himself, aristo-blond, a former double major in English and Theater who could sound warm and sensitive even when he was telling her to deal cutthroat, and so she figured she had no choice but to overlook those cum stains on the futon. If in fact they were cum stains, and if she was picking up other telltales. After all, her lickable G-lord was going for his SAG card, and that could make anyone crazy. Plus he gave her all the props for the angle she was working, the high end. The very thought sent him into falsetto Little Richard, "Sww-eeet Mag-<u>no</u>-lia," or down deep in the throat, "Lady Swee," in the style of some bebop player. She appreciated that, the validation, such as it was, and she had to admire the guy's range of voices. She only wished he'd come up with a nickname that wasn't out of a minstrel show.

Still, she'd never expected this. Never expected such bop out of Lady Swee. And her magic in the mall felt all the more bizarre after a morning when, at last, shit was getting real.

That morning, no sooner had Nola settled into her cubicle than she'd been knocked for a loop again. Look what popped up on her screen! Time to duck into the ladies' and murmur *sw-w-eeet!* At last the career had gotten real, right off the flow chart. The studio had decided it was time for an art project, a trip to the high end. They were ready to go with costumes and names and the whole *Titanic,* and for that kind of thing, who was their guy?

Madame Bovary, c'est moi. Or Madame Quality, anyway. She had her first honest-to-God shot at a property of her own.

So it's that very same day, the same dawn-of-a-star early lunch, when our Lady starts to visualize. Never anything like it. She's doing a Starbucks over at the Barnes & Noble, she's thinking maybe a novel, maybe one of those based-on-a-true-story, meantime sitting over a whole stack of books—candy-colored packages, Christmas under the tree—and no sooner does she get a picture in her head than it takes over. One moment she dips her tongue into the cream piled on top of her Venti, savoring, pondering, and the next a kind of extended opaque linguine has boiled up and out of those pages and started ribboning away in a flexing half-circle all around her, up in dancing pale Insta-Gro sprouts that multiply and fatten, up under her as well, hoisting Nola and her rickety 'Bucks table along with the rest of whatever this is, this sprouting linguine that unfolds out into the gasoline breezes over the mall and boulevard, all of it happening fast, lifting and widening with such balance and smoothness you'd think it was aware of insurance guidelines, and yet fast nevertheless, so that the store's second-shift manager barely has time to reach the Lady Swee, or reach where she used to be, her former reading nook, and it's only a matter of seconds really before this unfolding skyward and ribboning outward, these shafts of dream-matter or whatever, they start coming together as segments of colors and figures, yes you can see the forms taking shape across their gathering off-gray stalks as they start to link and overlap and assert themselves beyond the bookstore rooftop, beyond the fat windows and flimsy girders, until these eruptive rippling pieces of a picture reach their apogee and cohere into the grand retro shape of an oyster-shell drive-in screen, a massive open fan in place of the storefront, and playing across its semicircular sort-of canvas is the very movie our Lady had been trying to visualize.

She can sit where she is and watch it, the scene she'd had in mind (though in her happiness, as she'd tongued up her drink's white froth, she'd also thought of the better times with her G-guy...). She's got an excellent seat, actually, because the miracle moviehouse that's taken over an entire corner of this roadside turnout includes some kind of luxury box, a perch well up one slope of the fan. Up where you can feel the breeze off the Pacific. She hadn't realized she'd chosen a place so squarely in the LA flatlands, and till now she hadn't noticed that she was sharing her unobstructed view with the stunned afternoon manager of the bookstore.

This is a woman who, compared to Sweet Magnolia, has a little more color in her clothes but a lot less in her

face. She's blanching, and can you blame her? The last thing
a mid-level employee expects when she comes into work is
to find herself clinging, at early lunchtime, to a café table
and chair that seem perched on—*what* would you call this?
Nola sees the hatch-shell of a drive-in theater, but maybe the
manager sees the upper arc of a half-buried Ferris Wheel.
What would you call it, or call the FX trickery by which,
across this vast half-moon, there's playing a movie? It's all
the manager can manage just to glance over at the heads
and shoulders on the screen; to look down at the parking lot
makes her tremble where she stands, just as looking up must
stagger the rubberneckers below, taking cover behind their
open car doors. Farther off, out on the freeway, you can see
one fender-bender at least, while other drivers have pulled
undented to the shoulder and are coming out of their machines to try and get a handle on this weirdness, looming
up immensely in a fragment of a minute.

Plus what's on the screen establishes itself at once as an
intense business, near climax and in closeup, a man and a
woman in a riveting drama of love amid the turmoil of
history, their gazes narrow and tormented, their pouting
both full of deep thought and utterly kissable. Meanwhile
some inconceivable speaker system kicks in and we catch
a word or three of this couple's entanglement and despair:
Why can't people…this awful war.… Swee, looking on, needs
a long moment before she notices that the clothing's in-
consistent: something turn-of-the-previous-century about
the man's lapels and something thirty or forty years more
recent about the woman's collar.

And then, as our girl assesses these particulars, there
on an open-air balcony so high she can spot the sailboats

out beyond San Pedro, so far above the asphalt she'd break her neck if she fell—then as Nola thinks about Costume Design, just the sort of detail you've got to get right before you make your pitch, she understands with a flinching incontrovertibility that *she's the one who did this*, the Visualization that Ate the Mall. The certainty of it comes over her with a twinned surge, not only fright but also power, though a power in itself terrifying, from out of deepest left field, and under other circumstances it might've got her up from her chair and trying to have some fun with it, this wild hair; at least she might've danced in place. But what can she do here? Our Lady slips off her glasses, she rests a hinge against her lower lip, blinking, blinking. She hadn't even dressed the set. She hadn't pinned down the era. The image in her head hadn't come together, as yet, into anything dance-worthy.

She's still got to do her homework, okay, granted. But look at what she *has* done, the fender-bender out on the boulevard, the audience numbers growing. Clusters of onlookers came spilling, even, out of the armpit of the woman onscreen, where the doors to the Barnes & Noble used to be. Who wouldn't suck the stems right off their glasses to discover they had power like this, who wouldn't find themselves as much wound up as undone, tossed and turned in carnival giddies? Not our Nola, anyway, so whacked and fascinated that at first she doesn't notice, over her other shoulder, the closeups losing their focus; she catches the movie again only as the lovers do an elegant fade to shadow, to black, and then as their scene leaves its difficult questions hanging in the air the entire theater begins to collapse, the theater or the Ferris wheel, pulsing and shimmering

as again the mammoth half-circle separates into the fat silvery ribbons that had composed it, and insofar as Nola can
think at all she understands that her turn up in the crow's
nest is coming to an end, gently but not without alacrity,
her open-air balcony is wheeling down and around on a
receding surf of fresh-cooked pasta, the whole extrapola-
tion settling back into the café from which it came, the
girders and window frames of the bookstore re-emerging,
and the posters in the windows and the abandoned lattes
on the tables, the whole dull espresso-for-lunch setup re-
turning untroubled except for a Vaseline-like slick here or
there on the corners of the furniture.

That last, the leftover goop of Krazy Kat World, that
may be just the residue of her own dizziness, since after
all our Lady in her little black dress has been put back
into place with a certain courtesy, so that the same book
as before lies open on her tabletop. The title's slipped her
mind just now, surprise surprise. And she's not going to
remember, either, not while the manager on duty straight-
ens up beside her, regaining command of the second shift
with a chest-buckling gulp of nausea. There's no way our
Lady can deal with this woman beside her, her voice rather
like an eight-year-old's, insisting that *all in-store promotions*
need to be arranged at least *three weeks* in advance with the
Events Coordinator.

And that's only where the interrogation begins. In the
next half a minute Magnolia faces ten or a dozen more
folks rushing up and firing off questions. Naturally they
don't know who's responsible, all they can do is ask, but
what pains an industry girl the worst is to hear these hicks
straining to sound industry-savvy. As if her untrammeled

astonishment was only so much show business! These yo-
kels asking, like, was that *software*? Like, a tie-in with a Bo-
gart retrospective? Plus, wasn't the drive-in the totalizing
peak experience of American cinema, now degraded by
video and digital reproduction?

Our Lady's no longer so Swee, she's more PTSD. She
has no answers. At the first break in the helter-skelter she's
out of there, mumbling some excuse to the manager and
stuffing a klatch of fresh business cards in her purse. How
had she collected them so quickly, cards that claimed to
belong to writers, actors, production people pre- and post-,
cards that revealed no small investment in design and paper stock? How could there've been so many moviemakers
among the discount racks at the front of the store? Before
she'd lost the impossible scent in her nostrils, the smell of
gas and tar up half a hundred feet over the parking lot,
these wannabes were pressing their wallet-sized rectangles
into her palm—her gesture of blessing, she guesses. But
Nola has no miracles, neither for them nor for anyone else.
She can't begin to guess what book she'd opened, or what
page or magic word.

What her hand needs now is someone to hold it. Nola
needs her boyfriend, and in particular the part of him
that does Warm'n'Sensitive. But then by coming home
when she's not expected, when she's too upset to bother
with the garage, she winds up first having to deal with
some asshole who, it turns out after a minute or two, calls
himself Laverne.

She discovers the guy with his hands all over her G-lord,
the two young men coiled together giggling and whispering at one end of the futon, naked except for the new-

comer's disgusting eye shadow. An oily powder-blue like you'd see on some freak out of *Satyricon*, one of those mulattos Fellini always threw in somewhere (Laverne's dark, a caramel topping over G's Ivy League cream)—the lover's eye shadow stings the sharpest, a finicky veil draped over something just the opposite, over clutching and grinding absolute in its blunt rapacity. And Nola too feels like just the opposite, fumbling and confused, while these two were dead certain in their blood rush. That's what bothers her worst, the paint that fails to mask, that in fact highlights the true and ineradicable. It's far more disturbing than the final wave goodbye that Laverne gives his still-distended cock. The guy flips his russet meat first at his lunchtime trick and then at the so-called girlfriend, before he finishes pulling his pants back on (shorts, since G and Swee live a long way from those San Pedro breezes).

And after Laverne trots away, for minutes on end, Magnolia can hardly hear the things said by the man who remains. She can't tell the apologies from the rationalizations, something about something bound to happen sooner or later. Something about a conversation on their first date and the homoerotic subtext in Jerome Kern. She doesn't realize he's poured her a shot of Absolut Citron, chilled and neat, till she raises it to her lips. Maybe she tastes some Cointreau in there as well, a very civilized trank, and meanwhile he keeps at it, her well-spoken Gaylord, entirely presentable though naked above his unbelted ducks. God, he must've made the boys' mouths water. He seems to be arguing that it's better this way.

Nola, don't you see? They weren't working for the Peace Corps here. They were going for the mega-dollars and the metrosexual freedoms, and the sooner he and she came to an understanding, the better. Their relationship was a benefit to them both, certainly. Himself, in all of Hollywood he had no better pal than Sweet Magnolia, and nothing on the resume so useful as a girlfriend, either—an actor couldn't risk coming out before he got his card. But the two of them alone could hardly be expected to satisfy all their shadow selves. The last thing a pair of players needed were delusions about... about some totalizing peak experience...

The G has more to say, more wool to pull over the now-absent eyes of Laverne. Those painted yet candid eyes. Finally, though, with a whistling sigh and a silencing finger, the Lady gulps her biggest shot of courage yet and tells him there's something she's got to tell him.

And whatever he is to her now, a boyfriend or who knows, he proves in fact an excellent listener—well he'd *better*, hadn't he?—settling with one knee over the other at the same end of the futon at which she'd discovered him when she stumbled in. Gaylord inserts a thoughtful *hmm* now and again, always in the right place, and he makes a neat connection to classical mythology, the manifestations of Zeus or Apollo. When she takes a break from story-telling he's there with the reassurances, all therapeutic as he reminds her that there's nothing crazy about visualization. Nothing nutso. Anyone with a goal needs to picture it first, to establish its dimensions, before they plunge into the welter...

Oh, Gaylord, a hothouse flower so willing to share the warm spot. Never mind that he carried on with the same equanimity as half an hour earlier, when he'd been suggesting, between them, "a more open arrangement." Nola can hear that, she can see right through the man, yet nevertheless she finds herself nodding along when he says they've got to try it again. They've got to see if Miss Magnolia can do it again, the bookstore trick. If she could cast her shadows a hundred feet high, cast the spells she claimed she could, just think of what it would mean for the *career*. Just think of the elephant dollars, breaking into a stampede. G-Lord tucks right into it, as easily as he tucks in his J. Crew top. The Lady Swee has got to give it another try, and this time she's got to have a—a friend—there with his digital video.

She's nodding, yielding to the undertow. He and she come to understand without a word spoken about it that now they've got to turn on the news, the early show, the local. Our Lady finds herself thrown off by the anchorwoman's makeup, heavy on the eye shadow. But she picks up enough of the newscast to confirm, along with Her Man in the Closet, that no one managed to get a moving picture of this afternoon's craziness. A thousand video hawks in LA but none of them quick enough on the iPhone. The networks had to make do with a still that suggested a side view of an old riverboat, with the mall the body of the boat and Nola's magic theater the half of the paddlewheel that's up out of the water. You couldn't even tell that the two figures up on the screen wore costumes that didn't match. Besides that, the story ran at the close of the show, in the thirty seconds set aside for the Hey-Maude stories, Hey-Maude-Looka-This. Speculation had it that the quirky business had been intended as some sort of promotion, but since the technology had failed to come through as planned, the major studios were all denying any connection.

So what then for our Lady and her Lord, except to prepare for bed? She stumbles upon an appreciation of him as something else again: a person nearby in the night, a solidity amid the dim flapping laundry of the future. Plus this housemate always set up the espresso for the following morning. Nola discovers herself incapable of telling the guy to go spend the night with Laverne. She can't even say to him: Hey, you're the one who likes the *futon*. Rather, she counts on his reading between the lines, and she sees he gets the message in his choice of pajamas, long-legged and formal. Gaylord does up all the buttons too.

Still the girl stalls a while, as if the woven rattan of the bedroom chair has her caged. She might even be nattering. A couple of possibilities for an appointment occur to her, times when she and G could try out her new gift.

Wednesday p.m., Thursday a.m., mustn't dawdle. Another hour another elephant.

The next morning she tiptoes around behind ballooning personal boundaries, she can barely find the voice for *Have a nice day*, but then before her first espresso break Nola taps out an email for her accomplice. A couple more appointment possibilities. Gaylord proves likewise quick to make arrangements, both with the agency in the Hills and with the clearinghouse for under-the-table gigs. The following afternoon the two of them hit the highway, taking separate cars to a very different Barnes & Noble. A mall far upslope and inland, out where the Okies live. Still, the shelves hold the same chockablock narrative and the café sells the same milkshakes. It's their best opportunity, if you ask the G-Lord, and the uneasy star of the show has to agree. Their best shot is to recreate the same conditions while steering clear of anyone who was there the first time.

Urban sprawl is itself a kind of magic, thinks our Good Witch in Black. Wherever the city seeps outward it turns to forking byways, to spirals and cul-de-sacs, its roads change name and number and create, finally, the sort of asphalt bayous that hold the potential for reinvention without end. Case in point, the latest chameleonic turn in her, umm, her cinematographer or whoever. Gaylord tools into the bookstore lot in, umm, a fully loaded Hummer. He claims he borrowed the wheels from a friend, but Nola's been watching him for a while now, it's been almost a year, and today at last she could've told him: Brother, the car's the least of what you're going to get away with. Brother, you're fixing to steal yourself a whole 'nother *life*. This pretty young buck in his bling of a ride is going to grow up into a one-man showboat, a producer, a mogul—and multiple degrees of separation apart from his former Lady

In fact, he clambers down from the Humvee already giving orders. The G-lord declares, jabbing a finger in her face, that she ought to go into the store by herself: Sister, it's all about mood.

She adjusts her glasses, her smile. Since when did she need anyone to tell her how to daydream? Nonetheless she has to admit that, once you got this guy out of the bedroom and over where the deals are made, he amounted to a decent contact. A useful connection in a company town. After all, Nola first came to him as a new hire. Now as she works up her game face, she's thinking the same as he is, this swivel-hipped mover. She's thinking how whatever he gets on camera today could be huge for them both, viral and huge. As big a deal as Madonna on *Bandstand*, when the teenyboppers discovered the singer wasn't black.

Yeah, G, you get every last bit of bandwidth you can, and with that, *bon voyage, ma bête*. Take all your shadow selves and find another closet. As for the money, if she had to fight him, she could do that now.

Quick as a montage, she's settled in. The 'Bucks has plenty of open seats. In a mall like this she's a long way from a Venti and a madeleine, it's more like a Slurpee and Twizzlers, and her sophisticate's looks have drawn some glances. Every personality you put on demands its pound of flesh, doesn't it, especially here where the racks alongside the café, the front racks, are all Religious Interest. The Lady Swee can check the titles from where she sits, here *Glory on the Hilltop*, there *Stranger on the Roadway*. Yet the store should have no shortage of other titles, as well as plenty of customers who carry their title on a card: editor, foley man, continuity consultant. Every standing surface in the world bears its dog-eared layers of pretension. And what about her own surface, this table before her, covered with a fresh stack of titles? Embossed, half these titles. What about the way she's fallen again for their ridged and glittering promise? The first flip through her little library snatches Nola off into the not-unpleasant past, into that moment at ten or twelve years old when all things seemed to possess the same mystery, when she read as if seeping into the pores of story; and after that and a dollop of skim milk and French roast, lawd-a-mercy she's off again, she's riding the tepid but pliant stalks as they sprout, multiply, lengthen, as they take on hue and start to cohere, a flood of semi-liquids out of the agglomeration of paper before her, and it all bulks up at gusty and back-tightening hyperspeed till the whole behemoth of a halfshell is once more in place and she's at her perch at the upper curve of the mall-dwarfing movie screen (and this time she's alone, our Lady; whoever the store had on duty was too slow), and she can look up at today's contribution to the landscape, her latest spectacular, where the images haven't yet cohered, where she can't even pick out colors, but she's starting to get the voices: *You want to see?... You want to see?*

WRAP RAP TWO-STEP

C ome on, let me hear you, empty board up here. You
see the empty board. You know what we need. The
story starter, the first inkling, the concept on the back of
a business card. Now come on. And ah-one, and ah-two,
and...?

Tired, is that what I'm seeing, a whole lot of tired?
Just finding the auditorium was enough for one morning?
Sure, and back when the seminar started, you had the perfect project for this. You had the winner, the movie of your
dreams, with a narrative arc that curved overhead as clear
as a cable car over the fairgrounds, gliding along and nary a
hitch. Nary a hitch or a glitch all the way to sole screenplay
credit, and then to the gold for Best Original, and then to
a name above the title. Producer! *Executive* Producer! But
now that's gone, you've lost it, right here at the seminar.
We've been shouting at you too long. We've been shouting
all weekend, and come Sunday morning, it's practically a

miracle you could find the auditorium. It's the wrap session, the final, and you've got nothing left.

Really, you think I don't hear it, that whimpering in your head? That cryin'n'pleadin'?

Cryin'n'pleadin' won't do no good. I've heard it a hundred times, and every time, there's only one thing for it. I need to do some more *shouting*.

Come *on*. Empty *board* up here. Ah-one and ah-two.

You there, what? Smalltown America, the smalltown South, and? And a teenager, sure, teenage boy of a sensitive nature. Okay. Okay, and stop groaning, the rest of you. Don't I know it's a fallback? But sometimes it's a fallback and you land on a mattress full of money. I'm putting it on the board.

High school boy, not the most popular, and this single mom moves in next door. Single mom, and pretty, uh-huh. Doesn't escape the boy's notice, our sensitive boy, uh-huh. Even in the rental she's got, a three-room junker, a rust-garden lawn. First time our boy stops by he starts talking about going to college. The neighbor's a college girl, sure, an MA from NYU, no, an MFA, *Fine* Arts. Uh-huh. Just like that, our boy's all bright lights, big city.

Okay, I get it, Sprout. Don't forget I do this for a living. We all get it, everyone and his inner child, his inner thirteen-year-old. The kid sneaking around with a skin mag under his jacket. Anymore, don't forget, a kid doesn't need to sneak a magazine. Anymore, it's just a log-on, you dream up a name and check the box that says you're over twenty-one. But then there's you, my child, my outer child. You, now, you're going to go old school. You're going to write longhand. You remember the notebook we gave you the first day? Your seminar notebook? Uh-huh, nice, wasn't it, all those empty pages, and they're still empty, aren't they? Empty as a masturbator's mind. And it's time, now, you put something on that first empty page. Longhand, put it down: *Never confuse your movie with your fantasy.*

Lost in a fantasy, I mean, that's the masturbator. That's spending all day up in your cable car, up over the fairgrounds, riding back and forth. Back and forth and who gives a fuck? We sure don't, or we're not supposed to, here at the wrap session. The third day! We're supposed to be making a *movie.* Filling the board, nailing the pitch, thrilling the house. But a rookie mistake like getting lost in your fantasy? Don't you remember, the first day, we wouldn't even give you a Starbucks break till you'd learned the Starbucks Pitch. We whittled your pitch down so you could slip it between the order and the pick-up. Till it was all snug and money and fit on the back of a business card. And after lunch we took you straight into Title Scrabble. Title Scrabble, where the Z's no 10-point letter, not with *Biker Boyz, Venus Boyz, Boyz N the Hood,* not with *EZ Streets.* Not with *EZ Money* or *Attack Force Z* or *World War Z.* Or plain *Z* by itself.

Plus you've got to think different when it comes to the 2's. *2Fast 2Furious,* I mean, tip of the iceberg…

Okay, up there, in the balcony. You, yes, what? The neighbor, the new neighbor—you're saying she's black?

Interesting. Even post-Obama, you know, interesting. Balcony says she's black and, okay, on the board.

Well, we don't see so much empty space now, do we? And how about we double underline? How about we remember why you came to me in the first place? You signed up for this, not just the weekend but the wrap rap: Arc Mojo. After this, all you'll have is books out in the lobby, the seminar discount. After this it's Happy Hour. Happy, uh-huh, a whole hour. Jamba-lye, crawfish pie, fillay gumbo.

My children, this is your last, best chance. This right here, and take a look, the mess on the board is getting interesting. It's getting all the way to *To Kill a Mockingbird*. Or should I say, I mean I can hear you thinking, *To Fuck a Mockingbird*? I think even Helen Keller could hear it. Everyone's putting our Mayberry boyo together with his Sophisticated Lady. You, sure, down to my right. You spell it out. Evenin' in Dixie, waitin' on the levee, don' the moon look pretty...

Look, even post-Obama, it's still one of the best plays in the deck. Red Opie on black Hottie. Just look at the space it takes up on our wall. We're not riding any cable cars now. We're taking a chance in the hall of mirrors. In one reflection, you see something squatty as a munchkin, and then in the next, it's all high, wide, and handsome. It's a long way from just any old fantasy. It's handsome and light on its feet, and that's your bankable narrative, my children. If it's danceable it's bankable. It's what I like to call the two-step...

Excuse me, what, balcony? Up in the balcony, what, the *Koran*? Koranic Studies?

The Fine Arts, you're saying, that's the fallback. That's not enough. Our girl needs a degree with an edge.

Interesting. Koranic Studies, because I mean, she's dark already. She's dark and her book learning, I'm with you, it ought to have an edge. She ought to have a verse of the Koran tattooed above her heart. Cleavage that comes with a code. Plus, when she translates for our doofus hero, they're down in the back acreage. Wetlands, piney woods, fire ants.

Balcony, I am so with you, and the rest of you, come on, you get it, don't you? You *see* it, the space it takes up, on the board? It rocks us right out of the comfort zone. We take a woman of mystery and put her down in Plain'n'Simpleton. Come to think, she's got no visible means of support either, other than the permanent erection she gives the hayseed next door.

That's the way we roll. That's the two-step on the edge. My children, think about it, we're trying to catch an alien. The golden alien, the Oscar for Best Original, a creature with no eyes and no ears but a mighty big sword...

Okay, okay you, front and center. What? The woman's kid, you're saying, her love child?

A single mom, right, a girl next door who's been someone's Playmate. So her kid, it's a boy you're saying, we need to put that boy together with our cornpone. I get it. Our cornpone may not have a clue when it comes to the Dark Lady herself, but when it comes to her kid he's a buddy, he's a big brother. A natural. Our guy and her kid, there's sympathy there, a relationship.

Okay. Teachable moment. Let's see if we can use what we've learned since Friday.

My children, it's what I like to call the two-step, when our Catwoman's got a kid. I mean, it takes us from edge to heart, mystery to sympathy. Now, ah-one, ah-two...

In the good old summertime, we're ambling along with our Mama Mystery, and it's not like you don't notice her cleavage code. Not when she's in spaghetti straps. But to one side there's her new Daddy, he may be one dumb sucker but he's still a Daddy, because to the other there's her Lil' MacGuffin. I mean, that's what the kid is, isn't he? The kid's the question left dangling, isn't he, the cable car half off its hook? But we're ambling along with these three, down in the back acreage, down where the loam starts to get gushy, and our Papa surrogate, he's starting to play with her little clitoris...whoa! How'd I make that mistake? What was I thinking?

What, character and sympathy, is that nothing but sex? Ha ha, uh-huh, okay. Okay.

Settle down.

Cletus, that's better, that's the name we need here. Cletus, that's her little boy, and that's what our own boy's up to. He's playing with her Cletus. Settle down. We need a hick name, that's what I'm saying, and can't you hear it? *Good one, Cletus!*—can't you hear it? Carrying across the swamp every time the kid whacks another frog?

Now, as for what he uses to whack 'em, that's probably his father's old nine iron. Now, his father, that's the question. That's the MacGuffin. I do this for a living, boys and girls, and I know what's the question. But, as for teachable, that's names. Names are about the sympathy, I'm saying, maybe the sex but positively the sympathy. Your names need to pull up to the dock with all their signifiers aflutter. Think about it. Think about down in the boonies, down where you'll find these people, they've all got ribbons up. Pink ribbons, yellow ribbons, whatever. Always a ribbon tied to the biggest tree in the yard. Before you knock you've got to decode the color. Are these guys Pray for Peace or Kill Obama?

So, Cletus, that'll do us. In this movie, insofar as anyone's singing the lovesick blues, one way or another they're singing about Cletus. It's on the board.

But, Balcony, something else? What now?

Two names, you're saying, both for Our Lady of the Cutoffs. Okay, two, I'll set up a bracket.

One. Down among the frog-giggers, Mama's got her ribbons tied right, and she calls herself Sally. American as Spring Break. But, then, two. She had another name back in the noir. Back where it's all in code, MFA NYU, E train F train, there they knew her as Salem Shellac'em—I get it—the anti-liposuctionist. Leader of a terrorist cell.

My brother Balcony. Looks like someone's left the State Fair far behind. Looks *like* it.

Okay, brotherman, let's do this. Back before she left the wicked city, no, before she *fled*, I hear that, before she fled the urban experience, our girl had the cosmetic surgeons quaking. She wrought havoc across the waiting rooms. All that beige and gray, those calming tones, she hit 'em with tear gas and graffiti. Tagged 'em with SAVE THE CELLULITE. Good. Plus, what's that, what? Someone else? Don't everybody shout at once. Just, you're saying, she gives the docs a taste of their own medicine? Our lovely witch puts the surgeons on the table, she puts them under, and then she leaves another tag. No need for a toolkit, either, the doctors have all she needs. Okay. I mean, she's already got a tattoo, and isn't there an old folk song? Something like that? The girl who's been wronged leaves her mark on the man?

It's on the board, it's *half* the board, backstory.

Back...story, oh? Oh, that's funny, really? Somebody thinks it's funny, back like butt, like a butt that could use some surgery. Uh huh. I guess a few of us are starting Happy Hour early.

Settle down. Balcony, help me out here. We've got a terrorist body-conscious mid-Manhattan backstory...

Backstory backstory backstory. You can snicker all the way to the unemployment line. Who's running this session? Who's going to have time for your cryin'n'pleadin', after the guys with the checkbooks go thumbs-down on your concept, because your lead girl isn't *nice enough*? She's got to be nice, if she's the lead, and I mean genuinely. Inveterately. All part of what I like to call the two-step, and lately, you guys have been neglecting the one. The character half of the board, here, it's overshadowed by the noir. Way overshadowed. Salem Shellac'em the Sabotage Surgeon, going nasty on the boys in nip'n'tuck, she's nothing but nasty. Tear gas for the waiting room, chloroform for the doc, and how's that play with her little Cletus? With him and our lovesick Huckleberry?

I mean, ask yourself: why does a woman break away from the most fearsome anti-liposuctionist cell in Gotham and go live among the simple fisherfolk of NASCAR-istan?

What's up with *that*? Especially when, for a surrogate family, what she's got is a pair of pudd'nheads who like to catch frogs and throw them to the fire ants?

I'm telling you, I know the questions, and the answers need to include the truly nice. That's our two-step, first strangeness, then sympathy. First zone out, then zoom in, see the move? Come to think—Balcony, help me here—

we need it in the flashback, the warm'n'fuzzies, the high ideals of a High Yaller. So, what, again? Our girl had values? She reserved her punishment, I like it, she chose her targets. The most vain and rapacious. The Trumps and the Barbies and the doctors who, every time they take up a scalpel, first trace a dollar sign and let it bleed.

You got it. It's in the flashback—but wait, what? Some heartbreak kid? Something else for the flashback, you're telling me, a pretty little kid? Or pretty for a girl with a cleft lip and a clubfoot. Okay, one minute, I need to make some room up here. So, this kid, this girl. She's a desperate little freak. Nine years old max, and no need to shout, people. I see her hobbling into Dr. Moloch's. Down the hall, Salem, lurking. Black full-body leotard, okay, I hear that. Guy Fawkes mask. Then all at once she raises the mask. She's gaping, shattered, and she cups a hand to her earpiece. *Abort, repeat, abort!*

Okay, it's on the board, or pretty much. We're getting mighty crowded for a flashback. Getting mighty cranky for a wrap session, too, tired and cranky, but, what—you want to *keep going* with the flashback? You want the bad doc laid out on his own table? Our Camptown Lady stands over him with a hot needle, a whirring hot needle. Let it bleed. The dangling ties of her smock, you're saying, there's your ribbons. The glee with which she wrecks his data, slapping defibrillators against his hard drive and wrecking it with a single charge—there's your Title Scrabble!

Come on, settle down, no need to shout. Whyn't you try some reading? Whyn't you take a breather and try the book out in the lobby? It's all there, chapter and verse: the two-step. Your arc carries you away but also carries you

home, the refrain is reassuring, even if the end of the movie is
the end of the world. Even if the screen goes black on some
gargantuan space cricket rubbing its legs together. Still it's
the dreamsong of an American weekend, the thrum that
starts with Friday's first showtime, and it's the long and
short of why you came to me. It's what I was put here to
teach, the lullaby of the megaplex, the night language of
a nation.

Balcony, what, again? You say you've got it? The second
act, the arc's comeback—the father?

You've got the daddy to darling Cletus. Sometimes at
night when the cold winds moan. Though he's dark, same
as her, okay. You're the boss. The board, don't worry about
the board, I can erase and start over. This country, that
kind of thing, isn't it what we do best? So, okay: Daddy's
got a tat on his throat. A fragment, not the whole tattoo, just what shows above the collar. Though the collar's
mostly rags, sure, a filthy and threadbare set of surgical
scrubs. He must've worn it all the way down from New
York. Only place the aquamarine is still visible is against
the tattoo.

Except, what—it's not a tattoo? It's *fire ants*? Insects,
venomous, except in symbiosis…

ROYAL JELLY, PITCH & YAW

Silver Lake: The dream begins in incompatibility. How's that sound? How about we take you there, a place altogether different—incompatibility?

Venice: We know what it's like for you. All day you've got to listen to this stuff.

Silver Lake: All day long you've got to listen. People walk in and say, *We open on a country road, tumbling down the well of the headlights.*...They say, *We open in the city, smoke, drizzle, fire escapes, the figures amoebic...*

Venice: Not that we don't know how to open. Our first sequence, boom. Everyone thinks they know zombies, the zombie apocalypse. But what we've got, the way we open, I mean, not in their wildest dreams.

Silver Lake: Except, in dreams, that's where it begins, doesn't it—or shouldn't it, in dreams in all their incompatibility?

Venice: Like, a zombie wedding. Boom. A zombie wed-

ding, that's how we open. Beauty. We trash everyone's expectations.

Silver Lake: The expectations, the clichés, trash them all.
How many times do we have to come face to face with
a tottering corpse who was formerly our father? Our
wife or boyfriend or favorite child? With a knife in its
ear? Plus there are always the empty long shots. How
many times, a long pan of some empty public space, no
one in it except a couple of shambling undead.

Venice: It's over, it's *so over.* I mean, zombies have gone to
cable!

Silver Lake: Commercial cable, mark of the plague, might
as well carve the credits into a tombstone.

Venice: But we're off the wall and never before seen. We
open on a wedding, one look and anyone can tell. The
invitations. The gifts.

Silver Lake: The flowers, the right sort of flowers, and it's
children who hold the flowers. Children in full dress-
up, so many little brides and grooms—can't we pitch
that towards the strange? Can't the kids induce a chill?

Venice: It's going to get strange, as the camera keeps moving.

Silver Lake: The camera keeps tracking, and what are we
seeing, all these *disgusting corpselike* details?

Venice: An open neck wound above the tuxedo collar. And
there, in the knot of the tie, okay the four-in-hand can
be tricky, but that's a *finger...*

Silver Lake: And how long does it take for a pattern to
emerge? We're thinking, one long tracking shot and
everyone gets the picture—it's the groom's people. It's
the groom's lineup. How can you not notice, over
on his side of the altar, his side of the stairs? One

guy's standing on two stairs at once. One leg, what, how's this possible? Is he missing everything below the knee?

Venice: Now the girl, her side of the altar, her people, these are fresh-faced American kids. I mean, it's got to be the girl who isn't a zombie.

Silver Lake: How's this *possible*?

Venice: It's got to be, the girl saves the guy.

Silver Lake: The girl saves the guy. Isn't that the boat that floats? Isn't that Old Ironsides herself, sailing smack through the middle of our dream?

Venice: See, our concept's such a risk, big big risk, and the opening sequence goes right to the verge, the consummation, *you may kiss the bride....* You'd think you'd walked into an art film.

Silver Lake: But the romantic dynamic? The character arc? That'll float.

Venice: Always. The girl saves the guy. Always.

Silver Lake: Think of Endymion, one kiss from Goddess of the Moon, and he's youthful and beautiful forever. Isn't that what we've got here? Isn't that what our girl can do for her zombie?

Venice: For zombies *everywhere*.

Silver Lake: She's the center of our dynamic, the one who saves the guy and saves the world and does the explaining—at least until our big Reveal. You realize she's got to be some kind of scientist? A rare interdisciplinary specialist?

Venice: She's got chemistry, she's got botany, and, this is important, she's the only person in the world with a doctorate in the undead.

Silver Lake: With a woman like that, don't you see, it's best if we go darker? Latino, mixed race, always tossing her hair? It's best to add that layer.

Venice: Dead or alive, her and her guy come from different tribes. And then, *You may kiss the bride*! It's almost an art film. It's Juliet, *wherefore art...*?

Silver Lake: Because isn't she the fresh-faced Creole kid, or something, the one who saves the world? The one with, so to speak, a head on her shoulders? Hehhehhehhehhehhheh.

Venice: Ha-ha, ha-ha. We know what it's like for you, listening all day to this stuff. But listen to this. Next sequence, we take a big big bounce.

Silver Lake: When you open on a wedding, ask yourself, where's the last place you'd expect to go next? How about the *apocalypse*? We flash back.

Venice: Flashback to the apocalypse! Zombies on the march!

Silver Lake: What's the last thing you'd expect, just, *just* as he's about to kiss the bride?

Venice: As for just how far we flash back, hm. Maybe a couple of years. We think a couple of years, but that's your call. That's you and the test audience.

Silver Lake: Any audience, they'll never have seen anything like it, one moment he's about to kiss the bride, and the next, what is this, the essence of Meet Angry? The very avatar of Meet Angry? We flash back, and he's trying to eat her alive, she's trying to chop his head off.

Venice: Certainly no more than a couple of years back. Come the wedding, she's still got to be young and cute.

Silver Lake: She's going for his head, maybe she's got a hatchet, how's that for Angry?

Venice: The visual, it's eye-popping, ha-ha, ha-ha.

Silver Lake: Hehhehhehhehhehheh. But while these two are trying to kill each other, that's a major challenge for the exposition, isn't it? The backstory? Just imagine what our girl might have in her hand. Is it a hatchet, a pair of clippers, a letter opener? Whatever weapon she's brandishing, plus the way she using it, these have tell us something.

Venice: Thing is, we're in her greenhouse lab. Flashback to workspace, with ferns and Petri dishes. Degrees on the wall, chemistry and botany both. Plus this very weird doctorate in the undead. That's important, and also we need an old photo or two. Sepia tones, a hut, a kettle, Grandma or Great-Grandma.

Silver Lake: Aren't they both dark, the girl, the grandma? See how we cast the shadow of the exotic, even when we've got a scientist in her lab, working through lunch? Oh, and that's important, she's working through lunch.

Venice: It's all important. It's nothing you'd expect. Our girl's exotic and educated. Nothing like you saw the last time you sat through zombie love.

Silver Lake: We know what it's like for you, always remembering the last movie like the latest movie, putting the one up against the other.

Venice: But ours is nothing like the other. We sat through that last movie with zombie love too. Nice enough. Nice, but I already saw *American Graffiti*.

Silver Lake: We know what you need—there's no dream unless it's a new dream, and zombie love was last year. But when have you ever seen a lover like our Delta Lady? Exotic and educated and dedicated?

Venice: Working through lunch on her trial prescription.

Silver Lake: Working on a vaccine to save the world. It could be extract of Lil' John the Conqueroo. It could be out of Grandma's kettle.

Venice: Turbo-nutrients of Mojo Hand, could be, and then, once the zombie breaks in.... Oh, and don't forget just which zombie. Don't forget he's the future groom. We'll have an establishing shot.

Silver Lake: We'll have a recording device too. She makes notes while she's working, she does our explaining, because otherwise, honestly, who could keep up with the *changes?* How many times have you seen a sequence where, honestly, you don't know what's going to happen? Our girl doesn't fail to notice he's cute, either— she makes a note. But meanwhile he's trying to sink his teeth into her jugular!

Venice: In one hand she brings up the hatchet or the blade, and in the other she's got her lab-tested Eye of Newt.

Silver Lake: A visual dialectic, right there, psychedelic as well as dialectic. And did you forget she's at lunch? When our boy broke in, we were thinking, she'd be working on a platter of crayfish.

Venice: They eat the screen, crayfish. Plus, think of the fight choreography. Nobody can fail to notice this guy's cute. Trim, buff, and he's had the undertaker's facial besides, the kind of blush-on MJ used in "Thriller."

Silver Lake: "Thriller" could be useful in the choreography. The music wouldn't work, and not just because of the estate, what they'd ask for permissions. They'd ask the moon and the price of a limo round-trip—but artistically, aren't we in a different place?

Venice: Our concept and arc, they line up better with piano and strings. Especially after the girl throws the dust in his face.

Silver Lake: You see the beauty of it, the Lady or the Tiger, one hand full of death and the other full of cure? See the hesitation? A hesitation, and then she heaves the dust right in his face, Krakatoa!

Venice: We can go more FX or less. That's your call.

Silver Lake: Tea leaves, ashes, glints of mica.

Venice: She throws it, he snorts it, and boom, he falls on the crayfish.

Silver Lake: When's the last time you saw such a sequence? When you really didn't know? There's the hesitation, the inoculation, and he falls on the *crayfish.*

Venice: He wants the fish. The dead fish, not the living flesh. A change of diet, think about it. Think about the consequences.

Silver Lake: A paradigm shift throughout the totality of the zombie narrative.

Venice: We domesticate 'em. Their diet changes and everything changes.

Silver Lake: Have you ever seen anything like it? A sequence that sets you asking—what, *already? Already* the world is saved?

Venice: I mean, it's still only the first reel!

Silver Lake: Ah, "the first reel," a lovely anachronism.

Venice: I mean, just look at us *move.* A zombie wedding and then a fight tooth and nail, then we save the world and set up a mystery.

Silver Lake: A brace of mysteries. One, up in the old brown photo, doesn't that seem like someone we ought to know? And two, what was our world-saver thinking, when she went for that *third* Ph.D.?

Venice: Meantime, already we're on to the follow-up. We're going theory to application. Next sequence, domestication of the zombie. Put 'em to work.

Silver Lake: Remember, our Rappaccini's Daughter, she stopped her attacker with an herbal goofer. An antidote like that, you understand, we don't have to mess with needles? To get up close and pin them down and then inoculate?

Venice: We don't need some ex-wrestler pinning the zombies down. Our concept, it's wrestler-free. We're about a spray. A spray, and just listen to our visual.

Silver Lake: Yes, listen, we begin in an alley perhaps. A confined area, anyway—you picking up on how much room we leave for the director? You getting how much discretion he has, the backdrops, the choreography?

Venice: Could be an alley, or it could be, think about this, a movie theater. Think about going meta here.

Silver Lake: You picking up on the possibilities, the director could even go meta, screen a commentary on the folks before the screen...

Venice: Anyway it's a small space, confined area, and in there we've got our inoculation crew. Them, they've got the food set up. Crayfish, hot dogs, melon balls, cheese and crackers.... Actually, there's an argument to be made for pizza.

Silver Lake: Isn't there an opportunity in pizza? It's an eye-catcher to begin with, maybe a visual pun—all that red sauce? But additionally one thinks of Italy. Couldn't Southern Italy work as well as, say, Old

New Orleans? Places like that, don't they share the interracial conflation, the trans-oceanic interpenetration? Plus we like the possibility of going huge in Europe.

Venice: Your call, of course. Unions, distribution, the price of a limo round-trip, you know better than we do. What we know is, if we do Italy and pizza, then for the fight in the girl's greenhouse, before she hits him with the dose, we have to figure out something. We have to figure out how she ordered pizza in the middle of the zombie apocalypse.

Silver Lake: But isn't that our true calling? Isn't that why you invited us, to think of something, to rub these antiques till a genie pops out? Don't we *want* to be the first living-dead movie to break huge in Europe?

Venice: It's weird how zombies never took off in Europe. I mean, they went for *Avatar*. In *Avatar*, you've got a crip who marries a cartoon. You ask us, that's not so different from a zombie who marries a brainiac

Silver Lake: Isn't there a certain interpenetration? And wouldn't it just eat the screen, no less, if for the next sequence we went to a medieval hill town? Cobble stones, crooked alley, and there's our inoculation crew.

Venice: The pizzas are delivered, the boxes are opened. Picnic tables, maybe.

Silver Lake: Then there's the human bait, a track star, a lot of skin showing. And isn't she making a spectacle of herself? The way she keeps jogging around the piazza, chanting and sweating and spitting on the cobblestones, what self-respecting zombie could fail to notice?

Venice: They notice. They start coming. There's a wailing and a gnashing of teeth. But the jogger toddles calmly into the alley.

Silver Lake: When has anyone seen a sequence like this? A horde of the undead clamber into the alley, ravenous, merciless, and why don't the living in their path get a move on, why are they just standing there, fresh-faced, perhaps with a hint of a sneer—and what, *what* is that they're swinging up into action before them? What, bottles of spray, really?

Venice: They spray the baddies. The baddies fall on the pizza.

Silver Lake: When've you seen anything like it? When's the last time anyone came into your office and actually took you by surprise? But our metamorphoses, they're barely past the so-called first reel, and we've got tame zombies.

Venice: We've got Ghouls Gone Mild.

Silver Lake: And aren't the ambulatories still in one piece? Can't they still hoist and carry and put away? We've created a new labor force!

Venice: We domesticate 'em and put 'em to work.

Silver Lake: Can you see it, no exposition necessary, just one slow pan after another? Provocative color saturation? The zombies tote baskets down the rows of a vineyard. They truck carts along the aisles of the Amazon.com warehouse. They yank the levers on the molds for hard-rubber dog toys. Then there's children's toys— you wonder about those, perhaps?

Venice: Children's toys would need living workers. Quality control.

Silver Lake: See how our inspiration brings up one promising fillip after another? See how it keeps opening, unfolding, showing fresh colors? Let a hundred flowers bloom!

Venice: Our zombies need training too, basic training. A young woman with placards and the uglies in rows before her, groaning in unison.

Silver Lake: You wouldn't have much of a workforce without language, some rudiments of language, would you? Words of single syllables, gestures no one could confuse, doesn't our brainstorm have room for them all? And yet it never leaves the arc. Have you forgotten we've got a dynamic in place? The girl saves the guy, girl of color, guy in mortician's makeup. And, as a person of color, can't you imagine her *conflicts*?

Venice: She's got a hairball of conflicts. Grody dimensions, and it doesn't matter if she's Sicilian or Creole.

Silver Lake: Imagine, the camera pans across the zombie in her greenhouse, he's harmless now, he's a worker bee who can't even fly...

Venice: He can't fly, certainly can't sting, and the camera pans over him, sprinkling the manure or something, and then moves up to that photo over the desk of our Supergirl, or better yet a set of photos. Others of the family, all in sepia. Sepia photo stock, sepia subjects. Her ancestors look whipped, as if without that hoe in their hands they couldn't even stand upright.

Silver Lake: But mostly there's the grandmother—some sort of leader, isn't she? Every shot she's in, isn't there some sign of deference, the eyes lowered or the cap pulled off? Photos like these, that's the fun part, a fun project for the people in design.

Venice: Grandma's some sort of leader, yeah. But she's just a pair of arms like the rest of 'em, toting a kettle and wearing burlap.

Silver Lake: And is that a brand on the old woman's wrist? Our heroine, our girl with all the degrees, could she come of slave stock? She's a regular Georgina Washington Carver, on a fast track for the Nobel, that's in both Chemistry and Peace—and my God, what has she done, if not create another *slave race*?

Venice: A hairball of ferocious dimensions. She'd never have saved the world if she'd known it meant tearing out her roots.

Silver Lake: See how our vision can modulate? See how we take time for character? The pace has been breakneck and everyone can use a sequence in a lower gear, while our girl perhaps poles a raft into the bayou, Cajun country...

Venice: Or maybe she'll head for one of those Italian waddyacall'm. The elf-huts they've got there, the turrets with a beanie hat.

Silver Lake: And you know who she finds at home, don't you, humming amid the threads of simmer that rise from the kettle? Who else but Madame Laveaux or Strega Nonna or the very avatar of the botanist and chemist and doctorate of the undead? She might be long in the tooth but she's still easy on the eyes.

Venice: Mother knows best. Before long, the Old Wise One gets her visitor to admit she has feelings for her first case, her whaddycall'm, the first conversion. You know, Undead Worker #1. We'll have an establishing shot. The girl lowering her eyes. Blushing...

Silver Lake: Insofar as she *can* blush.

Venice: Anyway we keep it slow, a sequence for character. Closeup face, then closeup hands, and in her hands, a little bag of herbs.

Silver Lake: A bag, a word of advice, we'll take our time. But then, you understand, we're right back in the lab. Back up to speed, straight to the lab, now we're cooking. Montage. Leaf-clippers, eyedropper, Petri dishes. And don't we need one of those machines that whirl the test tubes around?

Venice: Always a great visual, whirling those test tubes around. It's hypnosis, think about it, and in this case it's our girl, she falls into a trance. She goes after her guy with the first dose out of the lab. Hits him right between the eyes.

Silver Lake: And you want a name director? You want someone whose very name says *ambience?* Then this is the sequence where you'll hook him, maybe you'll get Méliès himself back from the dead—because this is where you tell your director he'll have to show us a zombie in love.

Venice: Not that we don't have an idea or two ourselves. We see our Worker #1 for instance pausing over the laundry. There's a job for the zombie in your house, the laundry. But our guy, after his new dose, when he gets to some of the girl's things, brassieres, panties, we see him lingering.

Silver Lake: A zombie in love, honestly, doesn't that allow us a wild serendipity? Wild—and yet at the same time well within limits, PG-13? Well within conventions of a date flick.

Venice: We've got all that under control. All solidly this side of the R.

Silver Lake: You'll see how we handle it later on, but for now, think about this, what it looks like if our boy takes a special interest in her underwear, if he puts it to his mouth, if he takes a little gnaw...

Venice: A little kiss, a little gnaw. In this context it has a different significance.

Silver Lake: In this context, you point out any signifier, it'll have a different significance. Yet whatever your director works with, nibbling, nuzzling, whatever—by this point, can't we expect the audience to follow the dots? Our pretty lab magician has made her confession to the old Kitchen Magician. Our #1 Convert has put his face in his savior's panties. By this point, honestly, I have to ask. Doesn't everyone get it?

Venice: The girl saves the guy. Rudiments of language. Everybody gets it, and in five minutes' screen time we're back to the zombie wedding. Boom.

Silver Lake: We're back to a happy ending, our happy beginning, how's that sound? And out in the audience everyone's on board, though some of them, I'm sure you saw this coming, some of them out there must be wondering—wait, what? Happy ending *already*?

Venice: Some of them must be thinking, maybe I did wander into an art film.

Silver Lake: And they're wondering about a couple-three moments during those last five minutes. Weren't there a couple-three shots out of sync? A couple times there, didn't our lover boy bare his teeth? We were watching love bloom, the latest dose had made it bloom, somehow, some-who-knows-how, and so what was *that*, the lover boy baring his teeth? Even licking his *chops*?

Venice: The girl's showing more skin, too. I mean, a June wedding. And the way her undead crush is staring, uh, uh, that could be taken two ways. Could be romance, the way he's staring, uh, could be.... Then we come to the wedding, and on the groom's side of the aisle there's a lot of touching. The groom's side of the aisle, his crowd, they're clumsy, in need of a hand.

Silver Lake: And remember the altar steps? The Best Man, and the one with half a leg, and the one who left his finger in his tie? Those guys are all pressing the flesh, passing the ring, straightening up each other's monkey suits.

Venice: We could go more FX here. A director who knows his CGI, he could show us microbes leaping.

Silver Lake: You see how the new paradigm keeps unfolding? How even now there's another petal unfolding? This is the danger petal, a serious scare just in the way the groom smiles, as the preacher says *You may kiss...*

Venice: Wedding apocalypse. Boom.

Silver Lake: What about the side effects? Didn't anyone think about the who-knows-how *side effects*? But no one did, it appears, and certainly not our girl.

Venice: Whipping up the new prescription had her hypnotized.

Silver Lake: Her happy ending does a cartwheel straight into the end of the world!

Venice: The groom's people fall on the bride's. At least for some of the good guys, there's the aisle. There's the pews. Some of 'em have a little breathing room and a bit of protection.

Silver Lake: Except, protection—who's got none at all? Who's got no breathing room at all? You see where we're going with this?

Venice: The bride. The bride, she's up there right next to the groom. Arm in arm. The bastard's got his teeth in her as soon as she lifts the veil.

Silver Lake: Have you ever seen anything like it, cartwheel, apocalypse? The best person in the whole concept has gone whack! And doesn't that mean everything has to pick up fresh speed? A courageous few wrestle the girl away, by an eyelash, by a cat's whisker...

Venice: They get her back to the lab, but zombified.

Silver Lake: She's snarling, she's snapping, but they throw some church raiment over her. They wrap her in triple-ply swaddling. Can you picture it, blood and altar and miracle—chiaroscuro?

Venice: Anyway we've got to go darker here. We've got born-again zombies. I mean, there's no way to round them all up. No way the few wedding survivors can stop them, all the carriers of the flesh-eating side effect. A bunch of them, too many, wander off, they head scot-free down the church boulevard. We'll have an establishing shot.

Silver Lake: Every one of these newly reinfected and not-quite-dead is another horseman of the apocalypse.

Venice: Though the groom himself, he's in isolation. Carrier #1, the courageous few grabbed him too.

Silver Lake: And isn't this where we can look, briefly, like all the other zombie films? This, it's back to holocaust, and can't we borrow that look—famished, ravaged, perverse? Think about *Night of the Living Dead*, what it owed to the concentration camps, the photos from spring '45.

Venice: We're back to the bunker, the greenhouse lab. The prowling hordes outside, beyond the barbed wire, and the bride and groom inside, in separate cages. Of course the good guys have the spray, the original formula. But we've got that covered, a quick experiment with reinoculation. Another terrific visual.

Silver Lake: And another unfolding petal, namely, the zombie omnivore.

Venice: Reinoculate, they turn ravenous. All of sudden a pizza isn't nearly enough.

Silver Lake: Big Daddy Double Cheese and Triple Meat, it's not nearly enough, not even with a pitcher of beer and a bucket of ice cream.

Venice: Reinoculate and the zombie's a buzz saw. Cuts right through the kitchen.

Silver Lake: And where does that leave you? If you don't spray the undead they'll eat you. If you do they'll eat you out of house and home!

Venice: The spray won't save you, not after the side effects, and that's when someone realizes, they've got to go out to the swamp. To the cabin in the swamp or the hut with the beanie.

Silver Lake: Isn't the old woman the Ur figure? Happy ending or holocaust, our movie-going destiny, isn't it also her destiny? And she doesn't want it.

Venice: She wants no part of it. Maybe we'll have the witch brandish a poker, when the courageous few come knocking. Definitely she'll have a dog, an ugly mutt, toothy, a hound of hell. Looking a lot like a *zombie*, come to think.

Silver Lake: The Ancient, her roots deep in the earth, how will they budge her?

Venice: With an iPhone, is how. Product placement, Droid or iPhone, whichever cuts us the best deal and comes up with the best photos, the highest pixel count.

Silver Lake: Can't we move from face to photo again, a companion sequence, a parallel segue? A segue, this time, between Demeter and Persephone? The elder's a deep brown, firelit, while the girl, *her* girl, her acolyte, languishes in chains, glaring, a zombie, pale to the point of white.

Venice: A change sweeps over the old-timer. She quiets the hound and puts away her poker. We end in closeup, and for this shot, whoever we get, for this she's got to be the scariest thing in the movie. *I fix her,* she says, you understand she talks like a throwback, *but you not gon like it.*

Silver Lake: Now, let's take a minute, you and the two of us. Let's ask, when it comes to zombie fear, what's the base matter? The very bottom sediment?

Venice: You not gon like it, she says, and next scene, the Queen of the Underground has come to the lab. She's under the bright lights, and what she's set up, it's something else no one's ever seen.

Silver Lake: Isn't it, I mean the core and keel of it—isn't it incompatibility? Isn't it? Think about the very word "undead."

Venice: Ha-ha, ha-ha. The arc we've got, it *undoes* the undead.

Silver Lake: We've got a Black Magic Woman, but what she's set up, it's an OB/GYN clinic. In the middle of a zombie apocalypse! Who's the scientist now?

Venice: The story we've got, the science works both ways.

Silver Lake: And can't you just see our Weird Sister? She delivers the big Reveal as she ministers to her strapped-down Honeychile. And *Honeychile,* isn't that just the word, the nickname, for this low, sweet singing? Though our heroine, strapped to the table in what's left of her wedding dress, she's nothing like honey. They had to lash her feet to the stirrups. Old Isis croons in her ear, she springs the Reveal, but all her young votive can offer in response is a wailing and a gnashing of teeth.

Venice: The sequence won't be half over before the audience starts to connect the dots. This woman who saved the world, she always had a rare gift. The only grad student in a highly specialized field. The only person who'd ever for a minute look at a zombie and think, He's kinda cute...

Silver Lake: Our narrative, you see how it crests and dives and muscles on, so powerfully that we can trust the audience? Trust them to grasp that our Golden Girl is *zombie spawn?* Oh, and "spawn"—that's as far as we'll go.

Venice: We'll keep everything solidly this side of the R.

Silver Lake: A word like "spawn," like "insemination," that'll do. Why would we ever get out of the lab? What sort of a movie would get into all the greasy mechanics?

Venice: We'll keep it within limits. We know what you're buying, with that ticket.

Silver Lake: Why would we ever leave the lab? Isn't a euphemism or two in everyone's interest? Another word we'll probably use is "miscegenation."

Venice: If we wind up down in New Orleans, we want "miscegenation." In that context, it has a significance. Otherwise we'll keep things antiseptic, and we'll have our Voodoo Nurse whispering reassurances. Saying something like, *Honeychile, dis a lot easier for you den it was for me.*

Silver Lake: See how we can just hint at the mechanics? Aren't they just a matter of semantics? Then once our girl goes through the insemination, once she's a carrier of another kind, she's back to normal.

Venice: Any of the undead that come near her, after a minute they're normal too. Or abnormal, depending on your point of view. Either way it gives us another great sequence. All she has to do is stand out by the barbed wire and let the wind pick up her scent.

Silver Lake: The invisible majesty of pheromones, an Immaculate Conception, or in this case a Disinfection— isn't that the best way to handle the greasy, shivery, febrile particulars? To be sure, our girl's got something in her belly now. But isn't the outreach what matters, the power that emanates from the belly, the changes in every slavering creature caught in its ambience?

Venice: Every zombie, anyway. Think of the dance of the bees, how one guy comes back with claws full of pollen and the whole colony goes into a dance.

Silver Lake: Have you ever seen the dance of the bees? Could you ever have imagined that a few minutes watching Animal Planet would alter the base matter of the zombie dynamic? We've sailed the seas and come to bees.

Venice: It's a *colony*, the dead among us. It's life everlasting, except dead. It's the drones, hauling and picking and swabbing and pulling the levers. Only, sometimes they need a new queen. Sometimes they have to walk off the job with jaws snapping. It's not about feeding, it's about *breeding.*

Silver Lake: Have you ever seen a movie like it? Implanting the Royal Jelly of the undead? Our heroine, with what the Ancient whispers in her ear—it's like the movie of her own parents falling in love!

Venice: We could wrap up with another of those slow pans. High saturation, panning over the worker bees we never think twice about.

Silver Lake: Have you ever so enjoyed the end of the world? End of the world, in our case, comes to world without end. Can you picture it, the laborers placid in their labor, the Queen smiling down from the deck of her greenhouse?

Venice: We could put her in something like stadium seating, a touch of meta.

Silver Lake: Certainly it's been meta for our main girl, hasn't it, stumbling upon her very fate? Certainly she must be wondering—earlier, what was all that striving? The long nights over chemistry and botany and life and death. The trial and error in the lab, every experiment in six iterations, if not a dozen. What's the point in *striving*, when ultimately, all that you're about is this girlchild at your feet? An ordinary enough child.

Venice: Though she does look like she's about to bite her pet hamster in the neck. Ha-ha, ha-ha.

Silver Lake: Hehhehheeh. And what's the point of putting up a fuss? Isn't it better to simply let the spectacle unfold?

Venice: Just let the kid chomp. One last splash of adrenalin, that's what you're buying with the ticket.

BLINDED BY PAPARAZZI

A cherry role with a breakout actress. A choice opportunity, a major bump up from cable TV. Matty was
going big-screen while he was still young enough to do
loss of innocence. It made no difference that, within the
first minute of the phone call, he understood the project
was mostly about the actress. Spada, she was the breakout.
The studio, the brain trust, hadn't failed to notice how
much face-space she'd been getting. These days, while you
waited in checkout, Spada was the wallpaper.

Who was Matty to argue with the brain trust? *Brava
Spada*, he agreed, trying out the accent.

Born to break out, the double helix of her introns and
exons spiraling beautifully through first Libya and then
Sicily, the woman also had learned how to work it. She had
a practiced gaze, slantwise. The package added up to #7 on
some laddy-mag's list of World Babes, and—the news was
all over the wallpaper—she'd just left her boyfriend. Spada

had come into the Industry and left behind the Art, her b.f., one of those genius auteurs with a Citation for Excellence but hardly two quarters to rub together. Riding to the set on the back of a Vespa, she'd had enough of that. Maybe she'd had enough of those complicated Mediterranean types, too. Maybe Spada was ready for an All-American.

The thought crossed his mind, sure. To hook up with Spada fit the career chart neatly: first the cherry part and then the World Babe. It was about the work. If the studio had guessed right, if the multiplex was ready for cappuccino, then Matty would enjoy a significant bump up. This regardless of whether he and Spada started swapping orgasms. He'd like to get the girl, but as it was he'd got an epic.

Time travel. One movie, a dozen parts.

A typical sequence started with Spada the slave, Matty the master. He's the master with a heart of gold, hardly more than a boy when he took over his father's plantation. And his high-yaller house gal, her hand-me-down bodice a tad limp at the hem, she's been giving young Beauregard his bath since he was a pup. The people on the soundtrack came up with something crafty here, too, they synced the music so Spada's crooning keeps time with the droplets running down his hips and belly. Her lullaby itself a caress. But no sooner does Matty's innocence appear thoroughly lost than boom, big twist.

No sooner do they kiss than they go straight into that wavy-seaweed effect—some tricks never grow old—and come out of it into whole different seduction. The lovebirds go from a hot night in old Dixie to a steamy passage from the Book of Kings, a visit from the Nubian Queen.

This time Spada's the one with the whip. She's haughty with her young scribe. You might wonder just what part of Nubia this guy comes from, with his golden curls and sapphire eyes, but mostly you're watching the queen, rising regally from the scented water of her bath while the potted plants in the foreground keep everything PG-13 (some tricks just *never*...).

Yet once the queen and scribe move into the bedchamber, between the onyx and the ivory, it's not what you expect. She doesn't ask to see his quill. Rather, twist again, she understands she's fallen into a mystery. She scans the troubled gaze of her new b.f.

My secret heart, she declares, I see you feel as lost as I. Do you read the glyphs with such a gaze? And in all the chronicles, was there ever love so strange?

The boy sets his jackal earrings aclatter, shaking his head. He and his queen, he replies, appear to play across the millennia as moonlight sparkles on the surface of a pond.

The woman smiles but remains thoughtful. Then we must recall all that we can of the mystery from whence we came, she insists. We must delve beneath the golden inlay and leopard skin of this our present world. Only, first kiss me again....

And when they do, the seaweed billows back up. The soundtrack's got something wild going here, as well, thumb piano and piccolo. A ticklish new earworm for every pivot in the narrative. Now Matty slips a coin under his tongue in one era so that he can spend it in the next, now Spada scratches a graffito on a wall of the Coliseum, just before she's thrown to the lions, so that she'll get a flashback centuries later, when she visits the ruin as a nun.

Totally cherry! Besides all the changes Matty gets to play, the variety of accents and body language—and besides the opportunity to spend one intense hour after another with so knowing and supple an eyeful—besides all that, he's getting ten days in Rome. The brain trust figures they need to go on-location for the final sequence, the confrontation with the Emperor's evil Babylonian mage. The villain's got a ram's horn as twisted as he is. Blow the right note and it blasts a hole in the universal continuum, his rivals simply disappear...

The studio got the right man for that part too, one of those Royal Shakespeare coots who can do the Wicked Sorcerer with a flick of the eyebrow.

And chops like that, one flick and you're thanking the Academy, wasn't that really what this project was *about*? Wasn't it about the work? Matty would never have gotten this far if he'd left his career up to his curls and his dimples. Curls and dimples, any club girl out on Sunset had that much. He put in fresh hours with the voice coach, extra practice on timing. He enlisted the help of a couple of his old crew from USC, guys still in the business, happy to pitch in so long as Matty showed their screenplay to the right people. He did it, too; he kept it real.

But then early on in the filming—talk about real—the switcheroo from the movie came barreling into his life. Into his life and Spada's too, the uncanny came walloping, knocking them far and deep across the timeline. And there were no mics, no blocks, no crew. Matty may have caught a faraway blare of the Arkestra, a crescendo of sax, but that was something from the movie, something the people doing the sound had sampled for the players to help them prepare for the next scene. But when Matty heard it this time, he went straight into the impossible. And all he and Spada had done was step out for the evening. Her suggestion; she'd felt it would be good for "the choreography."

Were they going to dance? He might've asked, but before he got the chance, they were whisked away through fluttering kelp.

All they'd done was pose outside the restaurant. Part of the business, the buzz, and Spada wasted no time getting her smile in place, slantwise. It wasn't for Matty's sake alone, her bare shoulders, her lamé sack top, as if this were Bowie's first date with Iman. But then in the middle of the laser flash, that yellow Morse code, the two stuttered away, dah-dit-dah, into old trolley-riding LA, the LA of bungalows and Bakelite. When the visuals stabilized, Matty was wearing a fedora.

And when he spots the woman at his side he needs to confirm, blinking, frowning, that this was his exotic lead, because he'd never seen Spada looking so mannish or so white. He needs to remind himself that women's suits in those days tended towards the mannish, a lot of shoulder and no waist, though on second thought it strikes him as all the more bazook that Spada should be wearing a suit at all. Where'd her glam thing gone? And when did she get her skin bleached, a Dorothy Dandridge fade? Nonetheless this is Spada, as startled by the jump-cut as Matty himself. Doesn't take a sorcerer to see that, her looks all at once overripe. She's never been so easy to read, Spada, her face glowing beneath the tiger-pelt slashes of the shadows of the blinds. The rest of the set's underlit, the potted plants like black silk, but before Matty can get a decent look his date or his victim or whoever bursts into speech. She gives voice to a wordless and fitful music, full of pain it seems, yet bristling with sarcasm. A woman with a past, turning her pocketful of secrets inside out. Doesn't take a psychic to see that. Though Matty's nowhere near sure of himself, even as he tips back his hat and murmurs in hardboiled understanding. Really, understanding? Where'd he get this stuff? He couldn't recall seeing any pick-ups tacked onto the script. Not that he doesn't enjoy it when the woman seizes him in a trembling embrace. Not that he doesn't enjoy the notion that he's the last good man standing. Spada seizes him in a terror that might've left bruises, and her whimpering might be in Italian, and as they fall into a longing kiss the entire scene starts to tremble. They go to dissolve with no more than a hint of the rollicking seaweed.

And came back to the restaurant. They came back to empty salad plates, Matty and Spada, under a speaker playing "Moondance." The inevitable "Moondance," the greatest hit of white wine, and in fact on the table beside the plates there stood two nearly full glasses. Spada was likewise well into some anecdote, something that had to do with the photographers out at the entrance.

If she suffered surprise, dislocation, she took care of it with a gesture. She wiped away something on the air.

As for the wine, this hadn't been their first. Matty sensed the burring across the underside of his brains.

Intoxication, he recalled, used to work for the soothsayers. They had a swig or took a puff, and then the cosmos revealed its innards. Yeah well, not tonight. Not with the music in the background going from predictable to more so, Tony Bennett, and Spada was no help either. She allowed Matty to drive her back to the Chateau, but she offered zero to his attempts at making sense. What he had to say was mealy-mouthed, granted: *Did you notice...? Was that...?* Still, the woman didn't have to spend so much of the ride looking out the window, or where the window would've been if he'd had the top up. When she at last turned his way, at the drop-off, she revealed less. Spada gave him the full photogenic glitter, so that Matty's only fitting comeback could be more of the same. A grin like one billiard ball clicking off another.

He wound up with a club girl. A votive to help unveil the mystery. Over on Sunset he had no trouble scoring a serviceable bit of eye candy, but later, when they had a chance to talk, she creeped him out. When Matty found the words to describe what had happened, through the wormhole into *Chinatown*, the girl came back with some hand-me-down mumbo-jumbo about how the Divine always appeared in disguise. The Divine might spill its guts, but only beneath a duplicitous screen, a burning bush or the writing on the wall.

Creeped him out, utterly. In the morning Matty treated her to her favorite smoothie, but once again he found himself speaking in tongues. Out of nowhere, he announced that she would be his last club girl.

She didn't get it anyway. She told him she already had a b.f., on tour now, playing Jim Morrison.

Matty had others he could talk to. He had a therapist, no glamour-puss, a man who worked with the industry people who didn't buy into Scientology. He had his mom, back on Long Island, and he'd been planning to get in touch with her. He figured she needed to know about his upcoming scene as the sensitive Gestapo agent. Gestapo with a heart of gold, risking everything for the lovely half-caste who might be a spy.... And Mom, though she got her potato pancakes out of Fannie Farmer, had family that went back to the shtetls. But as soon as Matty got her on the phone, he found himself tongue-tied. He stumbled over the first euphemism, and they wound up covering old business, the danger of confusing the work with the life.

The mother asked, sympathetically: You remember Tom Cruise on *Oprah*? You remember him doing *Mission: Impossible* all over the woman's furniture?

Mom was great, actually. She and Matty hadn't gotten around to what he'd wanted to talk about, but they'd gotten somewhere. One good resonant *pong* on the sonar. By the time Matty came back on-set, by the time he slipped into his storm-trooper breeches, he knew that the person he had to do something about was Spada. This movie might change his life, and the nature of the change came down to Spada, and his mama hadn't raised a boy who couldn't suck it up and tell the truth when he had to. Tell it even when the person across the table was a jet-set hottie with higher billing. Spada was no more the Lord of Darkness than he was, and she could probably use a hamburger. Tonight, that's what Matty would suggest—he'd make the invitation—burgers and blues. Tonight he'd do something about the magic between them.

Then as he and Spada headed into a joint he knew of, The Bottom Feed, why shouldn't they pose for more pictures?

They took a moment outside the club door, enjoying the thump from inside, the tragicomic swing from A minor to B minor. They paused for the cameras, the lasers, and here it came again. The thing, the abracadabra. One moment Matty stood working up a *People*-worthy grin and the next he'd roiled through surf greenery into the middle of a chanting crowd.

His hair is down his shoulders (a good look for him, with these cheekbones) and he's chanting himself, his neck straining against the weight of a cast-iron peace medallion. Around his hips runs a fat rawhide belt with a hash pipe as a buckle. The crowd sounds angry and the air smells of chemicals, part pot and part worse, and he has no idea what they're protesting, he and this fine sistah beside him, her with the Foxy Brown 'do and the ragged jean mini. Are the two of them here about escalation or brutality? The Panthers or the Man? The Movement or the Wall? Matty can't sort it out, especially with that projectile kiting overhead, so colorful and yet so ominous, maybe a brick and maybe a canister, kiting across the sky and trailing an elongated flicker of cartoon-candy, cartoon-crumple, psychedelia. Now he spies the psychedelics everywhere, bristle and overlap, rotoscoping, except he never signed on for something like that, *Waking Life: The Sequel*. He must be tripping. Spada beside him must've licked the same tab. What else could've given her such a maniacal shimmy and pop, dancing the terror down, her chant smack on the groove? What else could've so bugged out her eyes? Talk about cartoons, her eyes call attention to how black she's become, practically cannibals-and-missionaries. She jerks like a Zulu.

Now he's warning her, pointing to the sky, somehow right on the beat himself though once again he can't be

sure of the words. Pigs, gas, guns, whatever, she's fright-
ened yet ecstatic, her own mouth not so much moving in
answer as framing a kiss, her arms spreading wide as if she
wants to be an easy target, because didn't she and her surfer
boy come together precisely in order to defy the machinery of death, the weapons of hate? And they go into the
clinch sloppy with inebriation…

So he came to. Popped out of the wormhole about as
much in the moment as a man can be. He was naked, Matty. Flushed with effort, slick with sweat.

He lay stretched out on the king-size, in her suite at the
Chateau. Out beyond the gauzy inner curtains dawn was
coming on. On Spada's side of the bed an iPod setup was
playing wordless Eurodisco, just audible, a weave of synth
and soprano as dense and exquisite as the woman's naked-
ness, here calling to mind a Sicilian olive, there suggesting
Niger River clay. Truth to tell, though, Matty wasn't certain he'd seen such things outside of the movies. Maybe
the olive in *The Godfather*, the clay in *Roots*.

In his bewilderment her color spun a towline. No resist-
ing how she reeled him in, this daughter of Mediterranean
fisher-folk, but as Matty got his hand on her he could tell
this wouldn't be their first go-round. He could hear it in
her luxuriant giggle, and he could see it in his excuse for
an erection. Spada should've had him solid as a bridge
girder. This wasn't their first time, and the tone of her giggle shifted. At that he groaned with unlikely pleasure, as
much aggravation as pleasure, and it made him think about,
of all things, the movie. He realized he should bring this
sensation, its tone and grimace, into one of his scenes. He'd
come back to the work, Matty. It was time to speak up.

Spada, what is this? We're traveling through time!

Strano, she agreed. *Un mistèro*, truly.

But she sat up unfazed. The actress went into lotus pos-
ture, so at peace about the bizarre itinerary she'd shared
with Matty that she struck him as more foreign than ever.
She spared him the indignity of a smile, but what could
he make of that pout? What, when it wasn't on the screen
or in the centerfold? Whenever a camera set her searching
for the best way to inhabit its framing, she went back to
some Mama or *Nonna* Matty couldn't begin to know. He
hugged his knees and became aware of Spada's perfume.
Opium.

The actress, so practiced at the line she spoke it art-
lessly, suggested they might be confusing their work with
their life.

Oh, *don't*, he said. Let's keep it real.

Real—eh. Then perhaps we are falling in love.

When she straightened her back, Matty didn't notice
her breasts so much as her muscle. When he shook his
head, it seemed only to get the perfume out of his nose.

Falling in love, she repeated. It's nothing to be ashamed of.

She wiped away something on the air. He ventured that
they were both professionals.

Eh. Two professionals who have an affair—what that
could do for the movie is hardly a mystery.

He agreed that the brain trust had an eye on the tab-
loids, when they brought Spada and him together.

Yes, but where do we have our eyes, *caro*? The windows
of the soul?

I'm scared, he said finally.

But perhaps we are only two people falling in love, going to the cinema. *Un film noir,* then *les hippies.* We go together, we kiss—

I'm *scared.* It's too *weird.* It's not what's best for the *movie.*

Spada gave it a moment, a beat beyond a moment, then shrugged. Somehow she shrugged and straightened her back at the same time, a combination impossible as her iPod's club mix in the brightening morning, and with that, to Matty, the two of them appeared terribly fragile. They might've been a pair of origami.

But when she noticed him staring, huddling, she had just the thing. She fixed up her gaze, slantwise.

They finished the movie, of course. Went ahead and had the affair, too. A woman like Spada, a man should have her while he's conscious. While he has his wits about him, and particularly when he's trying to learn all he can for the work. Couldn't go on doing loss of innocence forever. Besides, she was a lot more fun once they got to Rome. There the woman really came into her element, shining it on while the press went hysterical. They called him *Casanova d'America,* the headlines were everywhere, and during Matty and Spada's first night out together—she insisted on sharing a Vespa—they found themselves blinded by paparazzi. As the cameras went off, it did seem as if Matty and his g.f. were again somersaulted into a different time and place, an epoch of swords and robes and sand. Or it might've been an Easter spectacular. He and Spada might've been a couple of stock characters, the legionnaire struck down by the angel and the woman who discovers the tomb is empty. Who knows? The strangeness of experience, who knows? Matty figured he could wait till the final edits, and anyway by then he'd spent some hours on his own in the city. Done it incognito, in a Dodgers cap and earbuds (though in fact he had no music; the cord ran to an empty breast pocket). On foot for the aerobics, he'd hiked the Etruscan remains, the Imperial honeycomb, the ghetto from the Dark Ages, the Baroque overkill of the waterworks and the burly quadrangles of the Fascists, also cruising the memorial on Via Veneto for Fellini and *La Dolce Vita*. After all that, time travel—eh.

A SHRILL SKYPE IN THE NIGHT

Octopuses have been discovered tiptoeing with coconut-shell halves suctioned to their undersides, then reassembling the halves and disappearing inside for protection...

—NATIONAL GEOGRAPHIC NEWS, DEC. 2009

(*Text*) Have a look & then we troubleshoot.

(*Text reply*) 2 browsers open.

(*Text*) Time zone here, Perth, 16 hrs diff. Have a look. See what Im saying.

(*Text reply*) Search wds, OCTOPUS COCONUT.

— Oww, look. Just *look* at it, death of a dream.

— He's got it. I call from the far side of the world, I give his lonesome bed a shake, and he's got it. Reliable as bebop on the soundtrack in a wine bar.

— Callie. I realize we're estranged or something.

— No, *estranged*, that's married people. You and I just had this project. First a concept, then a meeting, then another meeting…

— A project. We made it that far at least.

— Don't I know it got weird?

— Mn, a movie project got weird. Adrift in the Dream Factory, I thought it was the Tunnel of Love.

— Isn't it an occupational hazard? First Mel and Callie hit on a concept, and next thing you know, they're whispering sweet nothings? Besides, bright side—didn't our creature turn into a feature? On paper we're still in development.

— Except, now this. The Multi-Touch display of death.

— You got it, you da man, even when a girl reaches out from the far side of the world...

— Cry havoc, off in the Outback.

— You da man, seeing what a girl's saying, right there on his screen.

— It's havoc. Google just those two words and you might as well put them on my tombstone.

— What? Tombstone? Mel, I mean, that's not the kind of talk I came looking for.

— She utters a shrill cry of warning, but it's too late. Already he's under the bulldozers.

— Okay now, lover, this kind of talk?

— Callie, it's our feature, our project—the movie I'd been trying to make since I left Galveston!

— This kind of apocalyptic mumbo-jumbo? Zombies on the horizon? This is exactly how, when it got weird, you made it weirder.

— Bad enough that my Callie Cuddles had to run off just when we'd gotten the green light.

— Here they come, lurching over the horizon, hungry for living flesh...

— Bad enough that, as soon as the thing becomes something, soon as the project gets to storyboards and mockups, she tells me she needs some space.

— Okay now, what I texted, I'm looking at it. "Trou-bleshoot," there it is, not a code word. Now, lover, can we lose this and do that?

— Troubleshoot. What I'm looking at is more like shoot to kill.

— Can we *lose* this? Can we go back to before it got weird? Used to be, with you and me, what mattered was the dream. We were Team Dream. Can't we go back? Can't we just look at what we're trying to make happen up on the *screen*?

— What I'm looking at is the AP, out of Sydney.

— Lover, remember, it's only a movie.

— The AP out of Sydney, put it on my tombstone. Baby, it was great while it lasted.

— Great days. You and me, lover, we were rolling in it. Haven't I got some of that right here in my hot little hand?

— Uh. Look, you did catch me in bed…

— The phone. Talking about the *phone* in my hand. The apps that reach to the ends of the earth.

— All right, give a guy a minute.

— Mega-meta-phone. Phonapalooza. And our team, our project, that's what *paid* for it.

— What? Oh.

— The advance? Are you forgetting what a score we made? They want to go 3-D on a creature feature!

— Sweet while it lasted. Every score was cherry.

— Plus, I hope you're not forgetting, we signed the voices. Don't we have the *voices*? With that kind of talent, this kind of concept—you see what I'm saying?

— Well, I used to. I used to see it. Baby, we had it all. But now, look at this ruination.

— Mel, I mean, how about reading between the lines?

— Tonight it's the AP out of Sydney, tomorrow it's the papers in Iowa. Next month, it's afterschool on National Geographic.

— But don't we have some wiggle room? You and me, lover, don't we have room to wiggle? We're in *development*.

— We are until they read the papers. Or whatever they read in LA these days.

— Plus we still have the voices.

— Yeah, yeah. The ever-popular handshake deal.

— We have *both* the voices. Male octopus and female. Naturalborn.

— Callie, tomorrow morning they'll call in the bulldozers. Same suits who gave us the advance, they'll bury us. Tomorrow morning, our badass octopus, Evil Itself with tentacles and a beak—he's going to be a *joke*.

— A happy denizen of the Great Barrier Reef.

— What came up on my browser, it's an octopus home movie. Makes me laugh even while it makes me cry.

— Look, don't you get it, I'm on it? I'm seeing the same streaming video, all that devastating domestic bliss, right here in my hand. Isn't he a diligent little critter?

— He ought to work at Home Depot. Even the word they use, "cephalopod."

— Anything but scary, and on top of that, are you getting this about the mate?

— Ozzie and Harriet, in their happy coconut home. Baby, it was nice while it lasted.

— Okay now, listen to yourself, Nightmare-on-Demand. I mean, whyn'tya ask instead, why'd she call?

She's out ten or a dozen clicks from the nearest decent espresso and still...

— Don't tell me that what you've got isn't the ruination of what we've got.

— Look, wasn't I married to that badass, myself?

— Eight arms, eight weapons. Tentacles of death.

— Plus, you cut off an arm, what good does that do? Cut off an arm and, thirty seconds of CGI, it grows right back. Genetic modification.

— Godzilla meets Goldfinger.

— We locked up the international market, too, totally. In India alone, can you imagine, with this concept? If there isn't some Hindu god already, I mean, after this movie they'd have to make one up.

— You know, it's still a trip, to think we were the first, the originals. No one else ever got past sharks.

— Mel, really, how many times do I have to explain? For anyone on the creative end, you put "octopus" together with "movie," there's only one name that comes to mind. There's only Ed Wood.

— Uh. This isn't helping, bringing up Ed Wood.

— You're not hearing what I'm seeing. Whyn'tya ask, why'd she text, what's between the lines? Lover, look at what we've got, the way we can wiggle.

— Just give a guy a minute.

— Don't you feel me, see what I'm saying, how we can get this *back*? Aren't we still in development? Don't we still have the voices?

— Mn. Interesting.

— So. You feel me? Is this a heads-up?

— So tomorrow morning, first thing, this is where

we're going—I'm the one who sends a heads-up.

   —   It's lucky I was hiking the Songlines.

   —   I'm sending the AP link to a select few. To the name that goes above the title.

   —   A name as big as that, honestly, it's no wonder he came up with a voice as good as that. A voice that stayed with me ten clicks out of Perth. I almost thought the man was born a mollusk.

   —   First thing tomorrow, he reads my post. About, here's the word. *Sympathy.* Our creature goes sweeter.

   —   Sympathy, sweet, there's the word.

   —   A kinder and gentler octopus.

   —   There, lover, yes there.

   —   It'll play in Iowa too.

   —   Okay now, ask yourself, haven't we worried enough about that? The people picking up their paper in Iowa? The big multiplex in Little America?

   —   Callie, I'm with you. This opportunity, I'm all over it.

   —   All over it? Then we're all the way back, aren't we, the whole team theme? It's you and me and our kindly cephalopod keepers of the undersea environment.

   —   Takes us into the family demographic, too.

   —   Is that what you're thinking, Mel, the box office? Me, I'm not thinking, I'm *dreaming.* Pure cinema. I'm looking at the voices. The voices we've got, they could soften up a little, couldn't they? Diminuendo: start vicious, go cranky.

   —   Plus the suits were just itching for more 3-D. This coconut cottage along the reef, for them it's the fantasy beyond fantasy.

   —   And can't you see it for the other voice?

— *Beyond* fantasy. She gets a character arc.

— Can't you grok the beauty of it, the bendy never-endingness of it, the superlunary concept? Our project was totally dying but with a cry in the night we slap on the paddles and defibrillate. It's adrenalined, it's flashing and yearning, it's bending and bending!

— Except, now this. Now you caught me in bed and we've got to finish what we started.

— The beauty of it! The project like an aborigine, and all we need to do is, we need to see the Songlines. You're asking where's the threat?

— What? Oh.

— Where's the threat, you're asking, when the ones with the beaks and tentacles have become the nice guys?

— I, yes, you've got me—tell me.

— I'm ahead of you there.

— Tell me, tell me.

— Because don't you think I came up with that same exact question? Out under a million stars and trolling through Google? It can get pretty intense.

— Intense. I'm shutting down my browsers.

— It can get so that anything is possible.

— Anything at all, alone in the dark.

— And it was at that exact kind of moment, same exact, when Stoly came up with what I needed.

— Stoly?

— Stoly, like the vodka, get it?

— Like the vodka?

— Are you getting an echo? How's your connection? You there?

— Mn. Stoly just came into the picture.

— Stoly, well, don't I have to call him something? The alpha male on the trail? Out here it's just Stoly, the stars, and the phone.

— A man like the vodka. Under a million stars.

— Exactly—you and me, we'd never need another meeting. One look at that video, that happy critter in its home, and haven't I got just what I need right here on the air mattress?

— The answer's right beside you. And far overhead, across the night sky, sketches form and disappear.

— Are you seeing what I'm saying? You and me, lover, we've got a new movie. Stoly came up with it. He's got this thing he does with the day's catch, he loses a finger in the mouth—funny out-there Outback thing. That's how he came up with it, exactly the threat, so exactly. I'm not even going to tell you. I'm going to text you. I'm going to show you the exact words, the ones to pass along tomorrow, the miraculous new movie.

(*Text*) ZOMBIE FISH
(*Text, same number*) Hello? Yo? See what Im saying?
(*Text reply*) We going to teach a zombie to fish?
(*Text*) LOL. But, so, see? You w/ me?
(*Text reply*) I see. The project.
(*Text*) New threat = total new arc.
(*Text reply*) Shutting down now. Tomorrow Im all about the name above the title.
(*Text*) Btfl.
(*Text reply*) The movie I've wanted all my life.

PLAYERS, TAWKERS, SPAWTS

L isten, I'm not saying you don't have a movie. Two girls and a guy and the Mars Rover, that's a movie. Come tomorrow morning, you pitch that right, you won't be riding this shuttle home empty-handed. You'll be riding a green light. I mean, if I've learned anything, I've learned to spot a viable pitch. The high concept, the balls and alacrity, the miracle no matter the demographic.

Still, the Flexxies—that's one strange demographic.

Yeah, strange, tomorrow. Pitching the Flexxies. So, tonight, listen. Listen to what happened with my project. There's time, a trip like this, and I think there's something to think about.

Anyway, don't they let you sleep in, out there? Come morning, anyway, you know you'll be wired. Try one of these, Botox and rye, and listen.

Now, my project, I realize that some of this won't be news. I realize you're flying the same charter I am. And my project, wasn't it blog-fodder, majorly? The gossip caromed from screen to satellite and back, again and again, ramifying. Of course that was before all the excitement about the Flexxies. But, we had a sports movie, right? Right. Sports movie, natural narrative—tawkin *spawts*. We had a natural-born winner about a team that never won.

That was key, the real world, that model. We had it set up so that an actual waking-life team would always be out there living the nightmare. Right from the storyboards this project was all about some genuine losing franchise, a bunch of bottom-dwellers, couldn't catch a break. Living the nightmare, I mean, natural narrative. Myself, you know, as soon as I flashed on the verisimilitude? I closed my eyes and I saw the green light.

No, I can't remember who they were, the team we started with. The Cubs, yeah, that'd be the natural. But for all I know it was a hockey team out of Mexico City. That's not my end of things. That's the research and, I mean, I'm the creative. If somebody wants to get into just which ball club it was, and just how bad their stats were, my eyes glaze over. What pops my eyes open is those first swoops and oblongs on the storyboard. I'm seeing it, the players and the people who stay with them, the heartbreak year after year. And this in real life! It's classic, it's stages of grief, totally.

See, the setup was, at first the players and the people who love them are all the nicest folks you could ever want to meet. It's a pigsty to you, but to them—paradise. Then one day Satan walks into the locker room and offers to help.

Telling you too much? I'm telling you too much? Hey, isn't that nice of you, getting worried about a brother's intellectual property rights. Thanks. Serious.

But what that tells me is, you don't know the whole story, the craziness of this project.

Listen. So some evil dude, "Satan" is a euphemism, he comes to our loser team and offers to help. Never mind what his wicked plan is, can't tell you that, but it works. The guys escape the cellar. The team begins to contend, big time— but. It's not the same. It's all hate now. The players and fans both tumble downhill in one big pigsty-shitball of hate. Finally our Best Actress in a Leading Role—and I mean, that's the kind of talent we got, I mean bankable, and she was a big help after the trouble started—anyway our Number-One Honey has to make a big speech in her low-rise jeans and tube top. An Oscar moment, majorly, and with that the whole community can straighten up and fly right. They can rid themselves of the Devil, drop back deep into the second division, and be the born losers that God intended. Both down on the field and up in the stands everyone works through the stages, the frank assessments et cetera, right up to acceptance, kiss, chorus, purple mountains majesty.

Classic. Stawwy I was bawwn to tell. Haw.

But, serious—we didn't have to pitch the thing more than once. Plus I told you about the kind of talent we got. And halfway into production we're beautiful, we're bankable, when all of a sudden the team we're working from, our model out in reality, the Mudville Life Sucks or whoever—that team takes the pennant. They won the pennant and the statuette. All of a sudden they're Clutch Cargo, it's craziness, right through the seventh game. Our long national nightmare is over.

Or theirs was over. Then there was ours, just beginning. The full colonoscopy.

No, no, don't tell me we should've changed the story. Don't tell me we should've retooled and come up with a happy ending. Are you forgetting I'm the creative? The miracle, I mean, that's my job. Anyway, don't you think we tried, my people and I? We went straight to the mattresses and put up the storyboards. Wasn't long before someone sketched out your basic happy-ending rom-com, either, like that Red Sox movie a few years back. They had a similar situation, that project, a team that went from outhouse to penthouse. And the way they handled it was, put the big comeback on the screen and have your stars run out onto the field, screaming for joy. Go Sawx. But! Our thing was different, it was the natural thing, real *life*. The one about the Red Sox, they were just looking for good times, everybody goes home and gets laid. Our thing was all about going deeper, further, the narrative without limit. No matter the demographic, we had to make it work, another layer in the mashup.

Brotherman, come to think—something else. Check the mirror behind the bar. Check it, yeah, see that? See how the Botox is working already? Haw!

Tomorrow, you want every edge you can get, with those freaks.

Now, so, my project. Things were looking ugly but we still had one significant piece of leverage. We had our Top Babe, I mean, there's a few things I can tell you about her without telling you too much. She was on the Madonna-to-J. Lo continuum. She hooked us into three or four demographics at once. I mean music plus fashion, plus our thing of course, and on top of all that she had sports. So when the trouble started she was solid. She's right there

about the narrative, thumbs down on winners, all about
the true-to-life and the tragic. None of that Hallmark Afterschool for her. She signed on because she wanted some
edge. And then comes one meeting, she's there in the War
Room with us and she's giving her thumbs down, and you
couldn't help but notice the woman's shoulders and pecs.
Her fashion line featured a lot of chest that season. We
couldn't help but notice, everyone in on the creative—the
fix was staring us in the face. We'd've been blind if we
didn't bring it up. And I don't mind saying, it was me, I'm
the one who mentioned chick sports.

Chick sports, I mean, staring us in the face. Our buff-
a-licious miss had competed herself, the Rollerblade Tri-
athalon or something, back in high school. And she could
see it too, right there in the War Room, and with that we
had our fresh angle.

A simple fix, actually, as these things go. Actually just
a matter of finding something else actual. I mean, losers in
waking life—the project would never work without one of
those. That was *sine qua non*, and I figure by now you don't
need a translation. Anyway we got research on it and they
found us a team in women's college basketball. Some small
college out in the Gunrack Hills. The girls there hadn't
won since the days when they wore skirts on court.

The school? I mean, they were only too happy, once
Production started handing out checks. They loved our
hottie too. They set her up with the coach, full access,
and our babe did her homework. She got her stretch, she
walked the talk, all the way out to the edge.

What? What, older—no no no. She didn't want to
play *older*. The woman knows our thing better than that.

She wanted to play *lesbian*. That could be the career, right there, the Lesbian in a Leading Role. Especially when, this time, the Satan who strolls into the locker room has to be a girl herself.

I mean, once again, we've got the pieces in place. We've got the scene on the shower-room floor, the coach in her practice shorts and sports bra, the final smackdown with the lady Satan. We've got the turnaround money. And then there was the ensemble. Unknowns, those girls, naturals. There were these two in particular, recruited from gymnastics, here on student visas. Out of, what was it, Burkina Faso? I know we called them the Rubber Band and the Square Knot. And girls like that, they gave us a strong secondary arc, see. They gave us fresh black faces in Wonder Bread country. You see that arc? We got Rubber Band married to the local minister at the Church of the Eternal Abortion Ban, I mean, talk about a strong second line. We got this super-athletic missionary housewife in her spandex spraying stain remover on a piece of laundry and shouting, "Begone, Demon! I command thee!"

So. We've got ignition, we've got liftoff—but. Suddenly out there in Bullet Hole, Oklahoma, where the story of the last winning season had long since passed into legend—you see where I'm going with this, don't you? See it all in hideous slow motion. An eleven-game winning streak, and then the playoffs, five more. Our little band of hicks, they sweep to the district title, the division championship. All of a sudden we're not the only camera crew on campus. All of a sudden it's another story entirely, it's Cinderella, and meantime we're back to the proctologist. Worse, while we're face down with our butt in the air, everyone else is high on a happy ending. Everyone in town has got a smile for us, a smile and a cheerful word: "Can't wait for the movie!"

Still, we're catching the games like everyone else. I mean, if we're out in the roadhouse, we're not there for the Possum Tortilla. We're there for strong rye and satellite reception. I mean, how else could we ever hope to catch a break, a fresh something or other? I mean, isn't it about faith, my brother? Faith, that's always got to be a part of this business, even when the ball starts taking those funny bounces.

Tomorrow, you know, I'm going to walk in there and pitch this project again. I watched all the games, I saw all the funny bounces, and tomorrow I'm going to walk that talk again. I just wonder how I didn't pick up on what was happening when I saw it on the widescreen. One of us should've picked up on it, somewhere during that craziness—how we were getting messed with.

But. Along about the Final Four, what we began to pick up, it was another vibe. It was the excitement every time those twin forwards out of Rwanda or somewhere came onscreen. You don't need me to tell you. You've developed the same nervous system. What we picked up was the rumble of a big narrative on the move—this could work—and we called LA. We called New York. Coast to coast, they were all saying the same, namely that those two girls ate the screen. They covered the court and ate the screen. Two fine young sistahs, their unis drenched with sweat and their hair gone nappy, and they were already under contract with Production. Then on our side, the creative, we knew what we had to do. We had to get out of town. Way out of town and over to Africa.

Our project, I'm saying, it was too real to die. Every time we moved, I mean, weren't we that much closer? All we needed was the least little bit of *traction*.

Of course this was all before we learned we were getting messed with. But, I'm saying—we thought America was the problem. America, land of damn opportunity, the goddamn national anthem itself all about a spangled show in the dark. A fresh fairy tale every time the ball's in play. And if the laws of probability are out the window, how can anyone make a movie? Your audience needs to recognize the Lord of Darkness at the first glimpse of smoke. They need to recognize winning or losing as it takes shape out beyond the second plot twist. After that they look forward to a comforting ascent, or a descent if you can find someone to bankroll a downer—anyway they count on it as soon as they see it coming on. The stages of grief or dying or lying or marriage or man or whatever. How else can you ever bring a bunch of strangers together in the dark?

The dark, like right there out the window, the *dark*. Right there's your Cineplex. Haw, a little irony, brother. But even out there, you set up the good probabilities, and the story fills even those seats.

So. Our project, this is how we came to see it—our project needed another country. A place where the wretched stay wretched. At the same time, though, we had to keep our talent in place. I'm talking about the leading lady here, the woman we referred to privately as our Check Magnet. Along about the Final Four, you can imagine, she'd been ready to bail. She'd been thinking, same as the rest of us, this'll never happen in America. But as soon as she heard the new mantra, location location location, she was back on board. She's, I can tell you this much—she's white. And she wants that edge, that stretch, right? So what could be better than Sistahs Without Bawdahs, plus some international pro bono? And I do mean Bono.

Capital B, haw, yeah. A little irony. It's just, that guy, he's always over in Africa, isn't he, and so the photo ops, they couldn't've been easier.

In the meantime, in the movie, our babe switched over to the super-athletic missionary wife. The role she was born to play. The scene where she condemns genital mutilation and then shows the African girls how to masturbate—that was genius, pure physical acting. That's going to show up on her cable bio some day.

But. But. Do I even need to say it? Out between the white lines there was never anything but craziness and funny bounces. We started out with basketball, maybe in Benin, maybe in Togo. But it was an Olympic year. And you know what the doctor says, while he's snapping on the gloves—just try and relax. The Benin Eleven, or was it the Togo Twelve, they took home the gold and we snuck out of town. We moved over to Burundi and field hockey. I mean in Burundi, forget about hockey, they don't even have *fields*. But, next thing you know, those girls are running around screaming after the last match for the World Cup. They're wrapping themselves in a Burundian flag three and four at a time and tumbling together to the ground. Made a great shot, these wriggling parti-color squealing happy choruses of many-headed human striving—but it wasn't a movie. Then next we thought we'd finally got it with Sudanese water polo, but I know you've heard about that one. Bono arranges to have a competition-sized pool put in (Bono, yeah, he always had the wrong end of the stick on our project), and after that, there's no story bigger than "the girls from Kurdufan."

Our Actress in a Leading Role, I'll tell you, I think it broke her. Our Project of the Dead, staggering from turn-around to turnaround, I think it sent her permanently back to music. Then again, this new CD of hers, it could be that she felt she owed it to the musicians. She'd brought some studio rats in on the project, pasty white LA creatures. It could be she felt she owed them, after all the time they lost working out first the school songs, then the National Anthems. No sooner did they get one down than they had to learn another.

Last call? Why, where's my head, that I didn't notice it was last call?

Brotherman, listen, here's the thing. Your project, I love it, it's action and character and one money shot after another, and if I were King of the Freeway, this'd be an automatic green light. That's how the story should end. That's one player to another. But. When you're in there making your pitch, if you need an extra wrinkle, you might take a look at that Mars Rover. You might want to see if you've got some stretch there, in the arc of the Rover—considering who's running the bank. This time we're pitching an alien culture. Alien bank.

I mean, Galaxy M31, that's a long way for a Flexxie to travel. Even when he's got his "gravitational influence" working, it's a long way to come. But our E.T., on first contact, he broke into the Industry. What's that about? He can manipulate the laws of gravity and the first thing he tries, what—it's *our* thing? One of those bus tours, the Hollywood Hills, "Map of the Stars"?

That's what you ought to think about.

I know you know the same as we all know about this. About the Flexxies, I mean, and how they've got to have drama. Drama, for them, it's a craving. It's their nutrition, it's their addiction, and I know you know that's not just the Industry talking. That's NASA. That's research, what was it—eight months? Nothing but very serious people in smocks. But what I'm telling you is, you're not going to need a smock, not after tonight.

Tomorrow you're going in there knowing the Flexxies better than anyone. You're going in knowing my project. The project, and what really happened with it—the way they were messing with us.

See, it's all about this Flexxies "influence," gravitational influence. It's all about what that meant they could mess with down on Earth. They had the influence, and they needed the drama—and so they created it. They stirred up what little they could. Mini-quotidian drama. They gave the ball some funny bounces.

Think about it. What they did on my project, a spin here and a bobble there, budging the ball a fraction of a fraction of an inch. But then, brotherman—then think about what you and I can do.

I mean, this influence they've got, couldn't you or I have developed the same? We could've done it easy. But we came equipped with better, with hands and feet, plus a tongue. These poor strange animules, way out here in the dark, you might say they're all tongue. Myself, I like to think they're all wand, one long wand. Invertebrate—

flexible, mos def. Still, for a wand, they're short on magic. They're a one-trick Flexxie, manipulating gravity, and that only just enough to put the wrong team in the winner's circle. Sometimes. Not even the smocks can say how long they were at it, contenting themselves with that kind of kidstuff, before they managed to poke out a few words on a keyboard.

Sentient beings. Contenting themselves with kidstuff.

You think about that, tomorrow, what you and I can do. The funkified narrative. The jeopardy and surprise. The slow burn, spin and rinse, startle and moil and vivify. Listen, that sports movie, my project? These days, one player to another, I've got no hard feelings. Naw. That's the job, it's supposed to get serendipitous on you, it's *supposed* to every once in a while put all of echoing creation through the spin and rinse. I mean, the Flexxies, they're amateurs. They came to us—you know, the Americans. They knew what it took to get our attention too. A trip like tonight, I'll tell you, I'd never do it without some very serious seed money.

And it's all according to Guild regulations. Travel, meals, and entertainment.

HOME'N'HOMER, PORTMANTEAU

A blank wall, I ask you—how's a girl supposed to act against a blank wall? How's she supposed to brandish a sword and growl an imprecation, when all she's facing is a big square sound-absorbent nothing?

Alya realized she worked in the Dream Factory. She was hanging in, at any rate, and long familiar with the improbabilities of the business, such as fighting to the death in club lipstick. Such as this soft-porn version of the Ionic chiton (*KIY*-tuhn, insisted the dialogue coach, *KIY*-tuhn). Years ago, on her first project, Alya had learned to brandish her cleavage as well as a weapon, give the fanboys what they want, even the S-&-M tease of struggling in chains (latex, no heavier than one of her kid's toys). But for this project she had to work with a *wall*. A convincing scream could be an actress's worst challenge, people didn't understand, but the only threat before her was the shadow of an X, a crosshairs projected on beige matte, a placeholder for a monster. X marks the monster—and this when the fear was supposed to be primal. The ogres under development, over in CGI, were supposed to loom up out of our muckiest pre-rational sediments. Out of the dawn of Western Civ.

Alya had every right to know where the killing blow might come from. She had every right to plausible fight choreography, even if it meant taking time from the shooting schedule. Her director, however, handled her as if he wasn't much more than a fanboy himself. One silver-tongued devil of a fanboy: *An actress of your caliber,* he'd murmur, *of your stature...*all beside the point, especially when you considered that flattery was in the job description for a director. His sweet nothings included the project's tagline for the press: *Part nanotech 3-D action-adventure, part date-night, chick-friendly.*

Okay, but Alya was the chick in question, she could still play nubile, hanging in, and a week into shooting she got her director to admit he hadn't read the book. Come on, he grumped, an adaptation. Okay, but if he'd known the original he could've provided a clearer sense of the dangers facing Alya and her romantic lead—and that guy was no help either. Seven years younger, a former Disney androgyne buffed up for the role, her co-star remained a cuddle-toy. In skirt and sandals, no less. A week into shooting, she had no option except to exercise what was left of her star power.

CGI lay just across the lot. Felt like another planet, granted, a world in which the sentient beings bore only a rough resemblance, pocked and untucked, to the men on her side of the galaxy. The nerd who opened the "Odd-eyes" file for Alya was just such an otherworldly creature, his comb apparently mistaken for a garden tool, plus this Zachary couldn't hide his crush on her. He couldn't even begin to hide it, his stare like the full moon, and beneath the moon curved its golden reflection, his wedding ring. You couldn't help but notice the ring, the poor guy didn't know what to do with his hands, and for a moment there the actress worried that the studio's go-cart had carried her back to high school. Was she going to wind up contending with an octopus, all grope and nibble? But as Zachary tweaked his software preferences, he regained his motor control, and Alya could suss out how, here on the Planet of the Function Keys, this get-together was a demonstration of *his* power. His wonkpower. She knew an invidious look when she saw one, and hadn't she seen more than one here in the labs, sharp looks, transparently invidious? The Morlocks had spun on their stools to watch her pass.

Then the man had the mockups open, the claws and wings and the wings with claws, plus the beaks and tentacles, and besides that a no-neck head on which, above a boxer's flattened nose, there bulged a single red-veined eye—and with all that popping open, on the biggest screen in the room, Alya left off fretting over the state of the guy's marriage or the degree of his Asperger's. This was about the work. About facing off against a critter as if you knew where the killing blow could come from, and she made a point of getting the names straight; you couldn't very well develop a decent choreography if you didn't know the enemy's name. Kharybdis, kay-*RIB*-dis, was that it, and what did you call this hulking one-eye over here? Pah, Polly, Polyphemus? One hellacious beastie by any name, that one, and she did wish she could see it move, she told her CGI guy, meantime indulging in feminine wiles, a dimpling, a simpering. She came up with a name for him, "Zak-Man," and with that he worked up further animation. She got to see how the wings would unfold from the shoulders, the claws unfold from the wings, and when one troll unleashed its triple-spiked tail, whipping it around a horned carapace, Alya tried out a bit of Thai mixed martial, maneuvers she'd picked up two or three projects back.

She came nowhere near her chaperone, but he was startled off his stool.

See but..., he said then, see but, I won, I wonder about a movie like this as a career move.

A movie like this? 3-D, CGI, FX? Cartoon action-adventure?

On the level of the career, see. I wonder, an actress of your caliber...

Don't you remember Meryl working with special effects? She did a whole scene with her neck in a spiral like Rubber Woman. Didn't you see that?

Meryl was Rubber Woman?

They've all got a movie like this. Meryl, Sissy, Uma. Cher, Goldie, Sigourney.

See but, the *Aliens* thing...

That was Sigourney, her franchise, totally.

I, I do get how this project is special. It's only *part* 3-D nanotech...

I know, right? Because has anyone done a movie like this? Think about it. Has any actress gotten a stretch like this?

The woman who wrote the Odyssey. *The Awe, Authoress of the Odyssey.*

The authoress of the Odyssey. Her secret has lasted a thousand years, three thousand, but now at last the truth comes out. We rip away her disguise.

Alya's one-man Geek Squad, averting his eyes, clambered back on his stool. She bit back a smirk: *Rip away her disguise?*

Aloud, she went on: Plus there's a mystery, right, a natural MacGuffin.

See but, that you even know that expression, "MacGuffin," see...

Who wrote the greatest poem in history? Who's the blind old cripple? Turns out it was a young Greek noblewoman!

Zachary kept his eyes on the screen, the latest hellspawn. You, you've read the book?

The two of them had met hardly half an hour ago, and already he sat there telling her about his dyslexia. Zachary could never make his way through a text so slow and antique, with words like "authoress"—but he assured her he was long familiar with the monsters, he wasn't *that* weird, and, see, hadn't Alya said something about getting a stretch? See, how about his stretch? His team was on board for the full gig, right through to any pickup scenes post-production, because in their corner of the industry, who wouldn't want to romp with terrors that were part of the, see, the *cultural inheritance?* Bad craziness, out of the pre-rational originally, yet now, like, *cardinal freaks?*

Plus a project like this, like action-tech, you, you know how they pay...

Yet to bring up the money sent him into diminuendo. Alya's new friend dipped his head, frowning, silent, and he twisted and twisted his ring.

She could suss things out. Behind her stork-like companion she could spy the room's eight-hundred-pound gorilla. The man was thinking of her divorce, to bring up the money brought up the divorce, the irreconcilable differences, everybody on the lot had heard, and on the next lot too, and the next and the next, and anywhere the news spread, anyone with half a brain could figure it was costing a bundle. Simply to return to her own home, this evening—that cost a *bundle*. That made a role as action-tech eye candy look like a career move.

Now Alya could soft-pedal her goodbyes, dimpling again for the Monster Wrangler. She could text her assistant a bland reminder about morning makeup. But both these people, like most of the players in town, kept the same gorilla on a leash. They knew what it cost to maintain a spread-wing home while at the same time grappling in the mud pit of child custody. The ex too could throw around some power. Nevertheless, once she got home, she enjoyed again the melody of the new security code. She could find the zen in throwing dinner together (tonight, pasta primavera) and eyeballing her pour (Falanghina), keeping it under six ounces. So too she got her warm'n'fuzzies with the kid, though tonight they only spoke via FaceTime. At least with Caller ID the ex didn't butt in, and afterward Alya crossed the house to the gym, thinking yoga but slipping, instead, into mixed martial. You go, girl. You got some *moves*, for those homunculi. Scaly old homunculi, they can't handle your moves. By the time the actress tottered back into her office, she might plop down at her desk and pull out some financials, she really needed to check those financials, but she couldn't make her way through a single transaction. She couldn't handle any computations more difficult than the pros and cons of sleeping in yoga wear. As for her pour of Grey Goose, the shot was a tad enhanced, the glass a gift from On the Rox, and later on, thinking back, trying to make sense, Alya understood she'd drifted off before her papers and laptop, there in the Aeron, before the monster hopped up onto her desk. She'd woken to find the creature scrabbling through a couple of quarterly statements.

Later on, thinking back, she recalled the vague notion that this must be a prank—sophisticated as all get-out and vicious beyond belief, a prank cooked up south of Satan—and yet she'd had that notion, a flicker of false illumination: this bastard on her desk could only be someone's idea of a joke. A rat-tailed, hook-nailed bastard, also mantis-armed, plate-faced, terrier-toothed, all no more than a foot high and scrabbling through her papers. One good eyeful and any better thinking was out the window, off along the migration lanes, and Alya was left with vague and impossible notions, or flashes of indignant aggro (those papers were *private*...), nothing in her head so potent as her screams, an office-full of screams, a double-wing-full, so that if she were getting punk'd she gave the joker just what he wanted, the total scaredy cat, though nothing so nimble as a cat, rather maybe a marionette in the hands of an epileptic. Her top rode up, her pants slipped down. If this were all a mean trick (and she wouldn't put it past her baby-faced lead, he'd never seen a piece of scenery he couldn't chew...), then Alya gave them such a bellowing funkadelic hopscotch, with so much skin showing, that the video would go viral before the echoes faded. At some point her screams cohered into threats: she'd call 911, she'd call the *service*, she had Mace, she had a hammer, a poker from the fireplace, and then her head cleared enough for her to find the biggest kitchen knife, a cleaver longer than the critter itself. Her panic relented enough for her to throw in a couple of moves—if she were on video she might as well show some moves— roundhouse from the left, from the right, not too shabby, at least it got the attention of the ogre nosing through her stuff. The little abortion hunkered down, there on the latest bank statement, you might even say it cowered, ducking behind its claws with its tail coiling around its, its ankles or whatever they were. Ugly little animule. Still it waited out her threats, her Thai aggro, it squatted over deposits and withdrawals like the worst nightmare of an audit, and finally Alya returned to her right mind, more or less. She could recognize the notion of a prank as insipid, totally, another insipid dream of how your real life must be elsewhere. The dream in which you're under observation and earning good grades.

Then came the low comedy with the neighbor.

Alya had neighbors, part of the script that she and the ex had been following. No ranch in Montana for them, no compound on Virgin Gorda, they lived in a *neighborhood*, they walked to the store, even if what they bought there were saffron and morels. Once in a while, too, they could gab over the fence. They could share a sack of tomatoes or a peek into another soul, and come a night when somebody sent up screams powerful enough to set the spoons and wineglasses tinkling, well, that person had neighbors.

Thank God—or, considering Alya's current project, *the gods*?—the face at her door turned out to be phlegmatic.

Decidedly phlegmatic, deeply wrinkled, the face of the widower who lived uphill, an industry long-timer who could always say he'd heard worse. He could play it like a trump: he'd seen so much back in Da Nang, everything else was No Thang. He'd caught a magic carpet to the States, he'd swooped down amid the other Vietnamese in sets and costume (they ran the union for years), and tonight was just another ripple in the ride. Just another white girl gone batshit, and never mind that she was wearing VC pajamas and a face that called to mind a napalm victim. As for the monster, it'd gone scoot. The gargoylino had shown off its leap at the first long syllable of the doorbell, *ahnnng-*, and it leaped, *-gehlll-l,* and it caromed farther, lamp to divan, legs dangling, you thought of a wasp with jet propulsion, and Alya might've been startled but she was done with screaming. As the creature scuttled behind the divan, she only let go a long, low syllable of her own, a sigh out of doo-wop.

After that, as she stood in the doorway before the refugee-made-good, well, talk about sets and costumes. Alya cloaked herself in a story. She kept her back to her house.

The neighbor took it quietly, his wrinkles staying put, though from time to time he brushed his thumb across his iPhone, keeping the screen aglow. You could see he'd brought up the speed dial, one touch would summon the police—and it was kind of the man that he'd come to her first. It was kind of him to think how it would look if she had a black'n'white show up at the house. The paparazzi had a sixth sense for this, a star with her head on a pike, but Alya lived alongside the local sachem, an *industry* sachem.

Thank God, or the gods. Yet even as she told him so, her smile genuine or almost, the actress stuck to her story. She insisted that tonight was about the work.

A convincing scream, she said, people don't understand, it's work.

Now it was his turn to sigh, more Delta than doo-wop.

You've been there. Never enough rehearsal, the budget is such a, a bogeyman. Now tonight, here, I'm sorry, but where else?

I've heard worse, he said.

The screen on his phone had gone dark.

A comedy, that encounter, call it *The Beggar at the Gate*, except Alya came away feeling as if she'd been the beggar and her neighbor had brought just what she needed. A cup of apathy, he'd brought her, because now, as her creepy stowaway re-emerged, wasting no time hopping back up on her desk, she went on past without breaking stride, making for the guest bath. In there she fished out the stub of a spliff from the baggie at the bottom of the ibuprofen jar, her assistant had a dispensary permit, and as she got her first toke she came back into the room and stretched out on the divan. If she'd had a feather boa she would've draped it around herself. She sipped on her spliff and sized up her new house pet.

And vice versa, insofar as she could tell where it was looking, this hybrid of rat and crab and hornet. Its triceratops head hung above the bookkeeping, long enough for the reluctant host to stop picturing herself with her throat torn open, or with dæmon larvae in her belly. Rather she fretted about her wrinkles. At this hour her dimples lost their charm, and the smoking didn't help, especially not month-old weed, stale enough to send her into a fit of coughing. By the time Alya got her next level breath, her hideous guest had returned to its invasion of her privacy. Pawing once more through her financials, its movements almost polite, it appeared to be concentrating. It extended a longer claw into a desk drawer and pincered out her checkbook. Alya was old school about the checkbook, too, she kept her own set of figures, and the drawer might've popped open during the earlier ruckus. In any case it was time to quench the spliff and drop it back in her baggie, time to fold the baggie back under the ibuprofen and run the bottle back into the guest bath (where a guest might've left it, see...). If there were any psychedelia stranger than a monster in your house, it was a monster with a CPA.

Its movements remained delicate over her scribbled math, and the actress saw no reason not to draw nearer. No reason not to study how the limbs and torso, if about ten times their size, might strike a killing blow. And look, lo—what was prophesied by Zachariah did come to pass!

Today's mockups, ka-*ching*! Look, lo, the wings, their veins and texture. So too the tail, the flex of the unused claws, these had an ugliness entirely familiar, as did the ribbing and abdomen. Alya fell into a bob and weave, her offense, her defense, taking full advantage of the synchronicity, her swami-nerd who'd seen the future. Because didn't every actress have a story like this? A career move that would never have happened without some mad synchronicity? They all had a story like this, some gift freak they'd known better than to look in the mouth, and Gwyneth had ended up with an Academy Award. A gilded dingus without hair or genitals, now there was a household monster

Alya could use, and so tonight she parried and kicked, she skipped and threw jabs, and she came up with questions.

Is that all you *got*?

The wee mooncalf once more raised its head.

Don't you want to rip out my guts, gnaw on my bones, and leave me nothing but a spot on the *floor*?

Its mandible retracted, almost sheepish.

Not that Alya could go on trying to read the thing's mind all night, not with the medical MJ burning in the throat and weighing on the brain. That Grey Goose in the freezer was calling: time to migrate. As for her ugly nocturnal emission here, she had plenty to keep it busy, a couple of scary notices about her investments for instance. And how about that photo album from before the breakup? She and the ex had kept a photo album, sure, printouts and stickum were part of the narrative, and now she dug the book from its hiding place and opened it across the mess on her desk. The shots from the Maldives, why not, she'd rocked that bikini. When some scum with a telephoto lens had caught her topless, when he'd sold the pics to TMZ, well, she'd rocked that too.

Through some miracle she made it to the far end of the bedroom wing, and after that insured herself hours upon hours of unconsciousness, setting her Droid on mute. She figured she retained star power enough to keep the studio from sending a gofer, for one morning anyway. And when Alya showed up on the lot, it was refreshed and without apology. She hid the chill of what she'd seen before leaving the house, the nips the bastard's claws had made in the photo album. The book wound up back where she'd buried it, of course, but before that she couldn't help but notice: divots, nibbles, nips, along the edges of a page or three. Also, on a bank alert about a recent withdrawal, itty cuts and slashes, as if her life were a whittle stick. The recollection gave her a chill, but she could hide the chill, she had enough to contend with right here on the sound stages, in particular her romantic lead. Her solicitous pretty boy: *Got your beauty rest? You feeling it, now?* If the kid had his druthers, she'd sleep longer than Snow White. He'd prefer just one name above the title, one set of abs flaunted against that blank screen, and come to think, wasn't that the worst of what Alya had to contend with? Wasn't that the fission core, that rectangle of dumb pale matte? High time she stood up on her hind legs and showed off her chops, what had she been doing since yesterday if not the work, the chops, and before the boy lost his concerned pout (adorable, Brando goes Disney), she was back in her chiton and cleavage. She had her dialogue, that had never been the problem, and the actress got her sword out, she began sketching Z's before a spot on the wall, and at that point the director had his nose in the latest budget report, but in half a minute he let the papers drop. He nudged aside the principal cameraman. The director needed to see this, a girl and her monster soaring to a height from which they could peer into the very goop of the Unconscious, and choreography wasn't even the word, not any longer, not the way Alya was feeling it, not the way she was *hearing* it, the director's new pitch to the press, another dream of another life taking shape as a murmur in her head, a burst of movieola patter, the words all insect segments, like "post-apocalyptic" or "Pixar-*Matrix*," "splatter-saga" or "aggro-buzz" or "B.O.-whammo," or maybe

"S-&-M-Whack-a-Mole," or then again "myth-o-matic,"
"freak-smack" or "Clyteme-nation," way past the old
school like "thumbs-up" or "topline," instead perhaps "nano-
alchemy," "wanna-palooza," "blog catnip," "retro-viral,"
"widget-able," "gawk'n'gag," or then again "Oscar-prime"
or "Oscar-pimp," or could be "3D-world," "world-boff,"
"world-preem," "world-whammo"...

When she came out of the scene the director got her
eyeball to eyeball. Loudly he announced that, next, they
were doing a full dragonslaying. A Scylla-slaying, and as
for the romantic lead, he should dial down.

What?, asked the boy. You want me to play *sidekick*?

His pout soured. Alya wanted to tell the kid the bile did
him good, it was his ticket out of the Mouseketeers, but she
didn't feel like getting her head bit off.

Besides, it wasn't any second-line player she needed
to speak with now. After the Scylla was slain, after she
was back at the makeup station getting the gore scrubbed
away, she had her assistant call over to the Geek Ghetto.
This time the nerd would get the go-cart, and wouldn't
you know it, just talking with Zachary left Alya's girl
with supernatural powers. Suddenly the assistant could
read minds. After the call the girl handed over a folder in
which, stashed among the documents, there lay a fat spliff
fresh from the dispensary.

As his cart pulled up, her bad-hair boy was on the
phone, the conversation intense. He had to use Alya's name
twice before he could ring off.

Awe, *awesome*, he declared. They're into a whole 3-D redo.

He kept hold of the phone, perhaps to keep from grab-
bing her.

They're back to the storyboards, he declared. Xena-*rific*, they're saying.

The guy wasn't a director, and this made his sweet talk that much more tasty. The folks from makeup were still in earshot, too.

Warrior Princess Queen of the Underworld. *Franchise-ready*.

Also Alya knew what the computer jockey got out of being seen with her, and why not indulge him? Why not soften him up?

Finally: Zachary, I ask you—where do you get your ideas?

Overhead, the floodlights had come on, and against the tarmac, the trailer siding, his shadow lengthened and hooked.

See but, Al, Alya, what? I told you I haven't read the book.

The book, well, a smart guy like you doesn't need to read it. Smart guy like you, you can imagine what it's like, for this woman. A gifted young woman.

You, you can tell where it's going.

A gifted woman in a gilded cage, what's she got except big, heroic ideas? No MacGuffin there.

The way he gripped his phone, you noticed his wedding band.

And the man who wrote the book, Alya went on, he's pretty transparent too, a geek who never got out of the library. One of those old Brit polymaths. But then there's you.

Behind him, his crooked shadow might've come out of a horror show.

Where do you get your ideas? Do you just close your eyes and, where are we, another world? Every day you face that blank wall.

Uhh, a blank screen...

She went on staring, narrowly, avid, while with his free hand the nerd fingered his ring, and though he'd switched the Droid to mute it kept blowing up, its message lights blooming across his narrow chest. When at last he spoke, what came out was distracted and clueless: cultural inheritance?

Nonetheless, the actress let it go. What further clarity did she need, when she had the guy's own breastbone, aglow with its Bat Signal? He didn't want to talk about it, her Zak-Man, he couldn't chase down that pill, because it led back behind the bones, into that breathless, bloody darkness with its throbbing omnivorous hulks, and after Alya had once more made her goodbyes, after she'd negotiated the traffic and the alarm and she was once more alone in the house, she knew just how to bring her night caller around. She knew how to get her papers scratched and gnawed on, her interiors tagged with rowdy graffiti. She might've started growing a claw herself, she had such a grip on her spliff while she dug for the sex tape. She didn't want the tape she was using to threaten the ex, no, but the one he'd never been able to find, the tape with her *previous* ex, plus a dose of X, not to mention an extra, a girl from On the Rox. That ought to interest the little troglodyte more than her financials, and she had better paperwork for it too, like the receipts for her abortions. She had the mug shot from when they'd busted the escort service. Alya had taken care of herself a long time before she had to take care of a child, indeed before anyone had called her Alya, and in the photo from the bust, the stare she was giving the officer in charge, she was making sure he got the message—if he gave her the mug shot, she'd be his freak—and she had the shot now, didn't she? She had rags and offal enough to occupy her nights for a lifetime, and with it, no end of outrageous promise.

CLOSING CREDITS FUN & COUNTERFORCE

S o you've seen what there is to see, start to finish, but you're still in your seat. Wasn't a great flick, no, that's not what brought you out—and anyway, didn't some smart guy sometime say that the movies were an art form based on how long a person could go without having to pee? Smart guy, and you can vouch for him after, what's it been here? Ninety minutes, a hundred? The movie had its limits and so does the old flesh and bones. Still, now that they're rolling the credits, you'll take a minute more. There was that recurring snatch of music, theme and descant, playful. Could've been Zappa, and let's nail that down, composer and title. Also, let's watch the fantasy die. Come the credits, everyone dies, even the assassin with half a dozen passports and a dusting of anthrax in each. Everyone collapses into a set of phonemes, white on black. The trickbag turns inside out: physical trainers and personal assistants and the crew in Wardrobe and Makeup. As for the zombies, these days there's a boutique operation out in the Valley. The fantasy falls into cemetery rows, names and brand names. Except, not this time.

This time you see the credits turn cannibal. They turn on each other, pieces tearing out pieces.

Is this a trick cooked up by the tech people? A joke? A joke would mean you've been watching a comedy. The comedies throw in a last gag as the screen goes black. They show the outtakes, interrupting the credits with the failures, like when the cameras caught some pretty boy in his Dodgers cap, though the scene was set in gladiatorial Rome. The outtakes, that trick, that's a risk, come to think. It can look as if the better laughs took place over in the real world.

Anyway, tonight, this might not've been a great flick, but it wasn't for laughs. That's not why you laid down eight or ten bucks. If all you'd wanted was a bit of diversion, you've got that at home, the smaller screens, the handy remotes. Hey, don't they call it a "joystick"?

Tonight, you came out for something bigger and more mindless. The full *in-the-round*. And look where you wound up, with credits that turn cannibal. Big letters that go all Godzilla on the little ones. You never realized the letter F posed such a threat, you never noticed its Tyrannosaur overbite, but here the F has erupted out of some perfectly well-behaved word, some tidy and justified line of print. Somehow the dinosaur DNA got in and the F has 'shroomed and gone carnivore. It's chomping out chunks of the rest and gobbling them down. It's not just tearing into the stuff up-screen, the information you might've gotten through already, if you gave two hoots, it's taking the attack *down-*

screen. Ripping away the recognition that's yet to come! Imagine the crushed hopes, for some fringe player in the industry. Some guy listed as Octopus Wrangler, maybe Tattoo Finagler, he's sitting in the theater waiting for just one name to scroll into view, and he glimpses its penumbra, the glow that peeks above the screen floor, the rising of the dream. His own immortal name. But then out of the black'n'white above, in a ruckus too fast to follow, this mass-murdering blind raptor of an F rears and snaps and tears it away.

Imagine the crush and bewilderment. Except, wow, you don't have to imagine. You're *there*. Shrinking in your seat, wondering about the people in tech, wondering about 3-D. Hullaballoo-cination.

There's the F run amok, and okay, F as in freak and fierce and fuck-all. But what's this one, an R? That letter's always seemed a peaceable galoot, the better half of purr. Look at it now, though, R as in fuck-*arr*, a capital that towers over the rest, galumphing around and using that long front strut like a tentacle. The letter yanks smaller ones out in clusters and scoops them up into its belly bulge. It's complicated. First the names and name fragments get plucked up and shoveled into a black belly, then inside that white outline the white nubbins cook down, in enzymes or something, and then as those crumbs of captured chalk evaporate the chalk outline around them grows denser. The breakdown of one seems to buttress the other. It's complicated, it's not uninteresting—and it's not even the weirdest thing. You've got the shreds of former signifiers frittering away inside the R's parabolic gut, and you've got an F ripping out dreams before they happen, and it looks as if the party's just beginning.

Also there's a kind of vacuum U, just look, a U wildly overgrown and schlupping down chunks of credits. Wherever the U rumbles into place, above it the rows of print start to tremble, for a while they resist, but soon there's some slippage, a little *a*, or is that an *@*, part of a logo or website. Once that piece drops into the maw beneath, into the rattling U, as in fuck U, other rivets start to give, the lines crumble, and there's that chalk circle of life again. The fallen frags evaporate, their cook-pot waxes stronger, and from there things only get crazier. In a couple of spots where the white flotsam and jetsam have been sucked away, the letters and what-have-you sucked into the big vowel's gape, whoosh, in a couple spots the black doesn't hold out either. Not only the credits themselves get vacuumed from the screen—also the credits' backdrop, the black, rips loose and tumbles into the vacuum. The very earth beneath our feet!

Or something like that, if you can picture our eyeballs having feet. It leaves you wondering: what's *underneath*? Behind the black, the border of our universe, if eight or ten bucks could buy you the universe—what?

Not much of the backdrop tears away, a scrap here and there, and beneath it the most you can make out is more scraps, fragments again, this time composed of color and jitter. Fire ants and Daisy Dukes? What are you watching? The movie, it could be, under there, where the black's been torn away. The flick you thought you came out to see. It could be, as you sort out a detail or two more, Kalashnikovs and synchronized swimming. It's something familiar, these tatters, these flashes where the black used to be. Granted, the edit is à la nutso. That slam dunk for the championship, it's so far out of sync, no way it could be the work of the people in tech. Still, whoever did this, they couldn't blast the entire multiplex to smithereens. They had to leave a few stretches of aqueduct above the ruins. And isn't that what you came out to see? A story with staying power? It's as if one of the monsters threw a wrench into the works and then the spit-out gears and bolts and sprockets came together as a better mechanism. Wrench-aissance.

Though you'd swear that no machinery could function long among these Zilla-Letters, these Destructo-Glyphs. They've got friends, more trouble. They've got three Ns running interference, when did that happen, one N pitching in with the F and the U, helping to pry loose a recalcitrant white bit here and there, and the other two running interference around the lumbering, tentacled R. Not quite so large, these auxiliary three. Not so monstrous, but no less of a menace to the lingering credits, the huddled names and brand names. Brand logos, websites, stubborn traces of a former reality. Stubborn, yes. They do appear to be hanging in, now that you've hung in, now as you get the larger picture.

They do appear, these bits and symbols here and there, to have banded together into a barricade. Or they've made themselves over as, what, a spiderweb? Lines of white print, or what used to be print, have wound themselves into thread and stitched back and forth across a patch of the confounding emergent movie.

When did *that* happen? How could it happen?

Wherever the backdrop came off, wherever the black split open and erupted in color and drama (isn't that drama, in those torn spaces?), the white bricabrac must've first been stripped. You couldn't tear out chunks of black, or the U couldn't, without first cleaning off the white. Yet there's some kind of comeback afoot. Some kind of resistance, that's the larger picture. The credits have mustered a counterforce. Those huddles are deliberate, that barricade is holding, and dinosaur DNA alone isn't enough to turn a few random letters into the Freaks that Devoured the Mall. They may have the size, but the others have the numbers. The others can shake loose of their rank and file, the torpor of reading left to right. A setup like that, left–right–left–right across the colorless flats, wasn't it ripe for plucking? Wasn't it bound to shred and crack and flinder and in the end, turn cannibal?

Now that the smaller critters have been set free, they can find ways around the marauding jumbos. Where the fabric of the former universe burst open, where there's an outbreak of story, no matter how bizarre and pyrotechnic, they can sling lines of containment.

Is the monster R in trouble? Is that what you're seeing, a brave squad of lowercase w's and h's, maybe a t or two, wrapping their arms around each other to create a kind of lasso? You never noticed that about letters before, how they've got arms, most of them, loving arms apparently, and extensible too. The way this squad links up, they might be taking that Sistine ceiling touch-of-God to the next level. They're a rope, a group-grope-rope, and they pitch their loop past the hench-Ns and around the fixed foot of the R. They yoke the big roughhouse and set him flailing and tottering. As it wobbles, wow, look, a few of the bits in its belly tumble out. You never thought of that, how the bastard may be huge but he's still two-dimensional, he's got his limits. He spills undigested nubbins of credit.

Elsewhere some of the advertising trademarks have woven a kind of barbed wire around the F. A cage for a Tyrannosaur? A mad experiment, homespun white wire, but then again, why not? If the credits birthed the Destroyer, can't they build a box to hold it? Some of those advertising trademarks were bristly to begin with, the people in Design wanted tension in the graphics, and meantime, over in another quadrant, other leftovers have come up with a tactic for the omnivorous vacuum U. A trick out of Three-Card Monte, bait and switch. First, a couple-three broken lines of phonemes will gather and compose themselves, as if they still added up to something comprehensible. Of course they don't—what you're seeing would never be mistaken for words in sequence—but nonetheless those few chameleonic lines will attract the U, eager as ever to schlup. It's not as if the big upright can *read*, after all. But no sooner is the urn in place than, above its hungry mouth, the ruse breaks and scatters. The signifier was only signifyin'.

The idea is, each time, you leave the freak vowel more run down. Doesn't even the Devourer get run down? Doesn't an anomaly, too, hit the wall? Anyway, what you're seeing is all a mad experiment. A counterforce of the blind, unsure of its end, it scrabbles on feeling its way.

It's a good thing you got out! Back home you'd have fallen into that stalling tactic, that channel-surfer's tactic, blipping from scene to scene in search of just the right shock on which to end. That notion that the right scene would set up your destiny. The dream that this country does best. Good thing you came out instead, you risked a doddering and fusty entertainment based on how long a person can go without having to pee. The flicks themselves have long since run out of surprises: if the assassin doesn't fall in love, the bookish girl in black whoops it up in a candy-colored romper room. There never was much opportunity for surprise, in ninety minutes or a hundred, and there's even less these days, when you need a multimillion-dollar urban-renewal package just to save the downtown moviehouse. The star-studded American shebang, winding up through the coming attractions and down through the credits in their grave-rows, that's long since been squeezed dry and shoehorned into smaller screens. Yet here you sit, putting off the bathroom. It feels like a stone in your belly, but that's nothing compared with what's going on in the belly of the R. It's mostly empty now, that upper-story belly, now that the rebels have lassoed its back foot. As the flabby consonant struggles against its leash, most of its half-digested bits and pieces tumble out. The remains, gnawed and pitted and in no way legible. But look, wow, the monster's stomach acids had a side effect. Look, a few of these nubbins have been infected. We're talking *zombie* nubbins, and they're sprouting up, too, muscling up. The alien spawn flex their dorsi, they spread their talons, and one of them's going after the rope that holds the mother-letter's leg. The resistance needs to regroup, and if they had any last semblance of jot and tittle, of names or logos, they've lost it now. Next thing you know, anything's possible, it's fresh dynamics altogether, here a Visigoth or a chimera, there a warrior saint or a comely stranger with a quick sword and a reflecting shield. Now when did that happen?

JOHN DOMINI is the author of two short story collections and three novels in print, as well as one book of collected essays. His fiction has appeared in *The Paris Review* and *Ploughshares*, and nonfiction in *GQ* and *The New York Times*. Grants include a fellowship from the National Endowment for the Arts. He makes his home in Des Moines, Iowa.